Disaster . . . or fate?

As I opened my locker a great cascade of books, papers, pencils, and rulers came shooting out. I tried to shut the door on them, but it was too late. I jumped to safety.

A guy who was passing wasn't so lucky. He put his hands to his head to defend himself from a flying French book, stepped on a loose sheet of paper, and fell down in the middle of the hall.

Ginger and I surveyed the scene in horror. The final sheets of my loose-leaf notebook were fluttering to rest around him. Other students were already rushing to his aid.

Shakily he got to his feet. He gazed around the crowd until his eyes settled on me. That was when I got my first good look at him. He had dark brown curly hair, the longest eyelashes I have ever seen, great muscles under a black tank top, and amazing blue eyes. He frowned at me and moved away with his group, leaving me standing in the middle of my own personal disaster area.

I stared after him, amazed. "Ginger, it's him," I stammered. "It's the guy I conjured up in your room!"

Roni's Dream
Boy

The Boyfriend Club ™

Roni's Dream Boy

Janet Quin-Harkin

Rainbow Bridge®
Troll Associates

Library of Congress Cataloging-in Publication Data

Quin-Harkin, Janet.
    Roni's dream boy / by Janet Quin-Harkin
        p.   cm.—(The Boyfriend Club : #2)
    Summary: Trying to blend in with the popular crowd at her new high school, Roni
hides her Mexican heritage, but discovers it's better to be true to herself.
    ISBN 0-8167-3415-1 (pbk.)
    [1. High schools—Fiction. 2. Schools—Fiction. 3. Mexican Americans—Fiction.
4. Friendship—Fiction.]   I. Title. II. Series: Quin-Harkin, Janet. Boyfriend Club : #2
P27.Q419Ro   1994
[Fic]—dc20
                                                                              93-50680

To Claire, with thanks for her great editing skills and her advice on Mexican-American family life. And also to her friend Yesi, for all her expertise.

1

We had only been joking when we started the Boyfriend Club. After all, a magnetic, dynamic person like me doesn't need the help of some little club. So when the subject of boys came up one Saturday night, I decided to play it cool.

We were sleeping over at Ginger's again: Karen, Justine, Ginger, and me. I'm Roni—officially Veronica Consuela Ruiz, but please don't ever call me that! The only person who calls me Veronica is my mom, when she's about to blow her top. I even enrolled at high school as Roni, which is probably why I ended up in guys' PE by mistake. But that's another story.

The four of us had been friends for about a month now, since we'd all met on our first day at Alta Mesa

High School in Phoenix. Ginger and I had known each other practically forever—we had been best friends since kindergarten. We'd been transferred to gigantic Alta Mesa when the city annexed our rural district of Oak Creek.

Sleeping over at Ginger's had already become a Saturday-night ritual for us. That night, Ginger's father and brother were both out, and having the house to ourselves had kind of gone to our heads. We had danced and sung along with the videos on MTV, using a big kitchen spoon as a microphone. Then we made popcorn, and I got to demonstrate one of my major skills—throwing popcorn up in the air and catching it in my mouth. Of course, everyone else had to try to do it, too, and pretty soon the kitchen floor was covered with popcorn. We were all laughing so much, it's lucky we didn't choke.

When we finally had the kitchen cleaned up, we went to Ginger's room, taking a plate of brownies—baked by Karen—a bag of M&M's, and a big jug of lemonade with us, in case we were attacked by hunger during the night. I lay back on my sleeping bag, watching in fascination as Justine rubbed white stuff all over her face. First she dabbed, then she patted, and then she slapped with the back of her hand under her chin.

"What are you doing?" I finally asked.

"This is a very expensive rejuvenating cream,"

Justine said. "My stepmother gets it from her spa in Santa Fe. She does this every night and she says it keeps her face young and beautiful. I'm making sure in advance that I don't get wrinkles."

I looked up and caught Ginger's grin.

"Rejuvenating cream, huh?" I said. "What if it makes you so young that you look like you're eight years old again?"

"What if you use it a few nights in a row and you turn back into a preschooler?" Ginger added.

Justine was used to our teasing. It was our way of keeping her in line. When we'd first met her, she was a total pain. She never stopped bragging about how rich her family was, and how great her old snobby boarding school had been. We were ready to strangle her! But later, when we got to know her a little better, we decided that maybe her life wasn't so hot. Her parents seemed to care more about money than about Justine, so how happy could she be? Ginger and I decided to see if we could whip Justine into shape. These days, she actually talked like a normal person. She could even be pretty nice when she tried.

"Shut up, you guys," she said now. "You wait until we're all thirty and I have a young face and you look like old witches."

"You always call your stepmother 'the witch,'" I reminded her. "And she looks great."

11

Justine frowned the way she always did when anyone talked about her stepmother. "So would you if you'd had that many face-lifts," she said.

"It was nice of your stepmother to let you use her cream," Karen said in her innocent way.

Something in Justine's face made me think her stepmother probably didn't know that she had it.

"Justine!" I cried. "You're asking for trouble."

Justine tossed back her hair, which was a sure sign that she was uncomfortable. "The witch has so much stuff, she won't even notice," she said. "Anyway, they're at a golf tournament in Palm Springs this weekend."

"Palm Springs," I said, flinging myself back onto my sleeping bag with a sigh. "That sounds so glamorous. Here we are stuck in Oak Creek, famed for its five-store shopping mall and its one traffic light, and the high point of our weekend has been popcorn tossing." I sat up again. "It's about time something fun happened around here."

"We still need boyfriends," Justine said. She had now finished with her face and was rubbing cream into her hands. "What happened to the Boyfriend Club?"

"That's right," Karen said. "We should be getting down to business instead of lying here doing nothing."

Immediately she pulled a pen and pad from her backpack. She set the pad on Ginger's bedside table and tapped on it with the pen. "This meeting of the Boyfriend Club will now come to order," she announced.

Instead of coming to order, whatever that meant, we all looked at each other and began to laugh. We couldn't help it—Karen looked so serious sitting behind the table, all ready to take notes.

"What's so funny?" she asked.

"You are," Ginger said.

"I don't get it," Karen insisted, but she was grinning now, too.

"Sorry, Karen. We're not really laughing at you," I said hastily. Karen wasn't used to being teased the way Ginger and I were. We'd been teasing each other since kindergarten, and Ginger's two big brothers had always made fun of both of us. But Karen was an only child, and her parents were far too strict to ever really kid around with her. Karen was used to being serious all the time.

"You just sound so official, Karen," I explained. "Next you'll be asking us to read the minutes of the last meeting."

"There weren't any minutes of our last meeting, were there?" Karen asked worriedly. "I'm sorry. Was I supposed to take them?"

"Give me a break, Karen," I said. "This Boyfriend Club thing wasn't meant to be serious, was it?"

"Sure it was," three voices said in unison.

I laughed nervously. "Do you really believe that we can successfully match up each of us with the guy of our dreams?"

"It worked for Ginger," Justine pointed out.

"Not really," I said. "Ginger's known Ben all her life—he's her brother's best friend. All we did was make her see that he was the right guy for her."

"And make him see that she was the right girl for him," Karen added.

Actually, all the Boyfriend Club had planned to do was to get Ginger looking so incredible that Ben would instantly realize he'd been blind to her beauty all those years. It worked, but not the way we'd planned. Ben had totally freaked out when he saw Ginger in her sexy dress at a party. But he'd also realized that he didn't want her dancing with other guys. The rest, as they say, was history.

"It's not as if we're really going together yet," Ginger said, blushing bright red. "We've been to a movie, and Ben does hold my hand, but that's as far as we've gotten."

"Sounds good to me," Karen said. "I'd settle for a cute guy holding my hand and taking me to a movie, if I could just figure out how to meet one."

"That's what the club is supposed to do," Justine said. "We agreed that four heads were better than one. All we have to do is come up with ways to meet guys."

14

"We've tried, and each time has been a horrible failure," I said. "We tried cheerleading. We went to the most embarrassing freshman dance in history. We gave a party that was a total disaster. I even signed up for guys' PE. I don't know what else we can do."

"There's always the nerds," Ginger said.

"Please! We're talking about the men of our dreams, not our nightmares," I said. A group of geeky guys had latched on to us the first day of school, and they still thought they could win us over with their charm. We tried to avoid them whenever possible, but they had a knack for showing up at the most embarrassing moments.

"It is hard to meet guys," Karen said. "I still think we should check out the clubs at school. Guys have to do something with their spare time. And all the advice columns tell you that romance blossoms when you share interests."

Ginger and I giggled.

"I'm not even sure what *my* interests are," Ginger said. "There are so many new things to try—computers, the radio station, service clubs . . ."

"My number-one interest right now is meeting guys," I said.

"Mine too," Justine agreed. "Of course, at Sagebrush Academy, there was no problem—"

"They flew in the most popular guys from Hollywood for the weekend?" Karen quipped.

15

"I was going to say that we had regular dances with the guys' school across the valley, and those boys were all hunks. That's more than I can say for the freshman class of Alta Mesa."

"I don't see why we should only be looking at freshmen," I said. "I wouldn't mind a cute sophomore, or even a junior. You know, boys don't mature as fast as we do."

"Don't set your sights too high, Roni," Justine said. "Maybe if you were cultured and had expensive clothes like me . . ."

"Thanks for the vote of confidence, Justine," I said.

"I think Karen's right about checking out the clubs," Ginger interrupted hastily. She knows how easily Justine can make me mad. "That's one of the good things about a school the size of Alta Mesa. There are hundreds of clubs. Some of them must attract cute guys."

"Maybe there's a Boyfriend Club at school!" Justine suggested.

"Yeah, right!" I said, laughing.

"We could make ours official," Ginger suggested.

"Can you see Principal Lazarow giving his official blessing to a dating service?" I asked.

"It's not a dating service," Karen said primly. "It's a scientific society to study and further the social interaction between the sexes."

"And what exactly is that?" Justine demanded.

"A dating service."

"There must be some clubs that provide the right atmosphere to meet guys," Ginger said thoughtfully.

"The problem is that most of the good clubs meet after school," I said. "My mom worries that I'll miss the last bus home."

Karen nodded. "I know," she said. "My parents worry that after-school activities will get in the way of my violin practice. I'm glad one of my friends has strict parents like mine."

Karen and I both suffered from parents with very old-fashioned ideas. This hadn't mattered to me at my previous school, because half the kids were from Mexican-American backgrounds like me, and they all had to put up with parents who had strange ideas about dress and hairstyles. But now that we were at a school where there were almost no minorities, I stood out like a sore thumb in the old-fashioned skirts my mom made me wear. I have to admit that I usually changed into normal clothes before I got to school. But just *looking* normal never made me feel like I really fit in at Alta Mesa.

Ginger jumped up suddenly. "You guys should come to the Pop Warner game with me tomorrow!" she said.

"Pop Warner?" Justine looked horrified. "Isn't that like Little League?"

"Ginger, I know we're desperate to meet guys,"

Karen said. "But I'm not so desperate that I want to date a ten-year-old."

"No, listen," Ginger said. "I'm going because Ben is one of the coaches."

"Aha," I said. "Now we understand the sudden interest in three-foot-tall quarterbacks."

Ginger blushed again. These days, any mention of Ben made a dreamy look come into her eyes, and any teasing about him made her blush. It was really annoying.

"What I was trying to say," she said loudly, "is that quite a few high school guys show up to cheer on their old teams or to help their little brothers."

"Hey, that's not such a bad idea," Justine said. "I might come with you, Ginger. I have nothing else to do tomorrow."

"I have violin lessons tomorrow," Karen said sadly.

"Roni? Want to come to the football game with us?" Ginger asked.

I shook my head. "I can't go anywhere tomorrow. My *abuela* is coming."

"Your what?" Justine asked.

Now it was my turn to blush. Why did I always forget the English word for grandmother? Maybe it was because she was only referred to as Abuela or Abuelita in our house.

"My grandmother is coming," I said. "She comes

to stay with us once a year when my aunt Luisa goes on vacation."

"How nice for you," Karen said.

I must have made a face, because she asked, "Isn't it nice? I wish I had a grandmother who would come visit me. One of mine is dead and the other is in Vietnam. I've never met her."

"Abuela's nice enough," I said slowly. "It's just that . . ."

"What?" Justine asked.

"She's different. She speaks only Spanish, for one thing, so we all have to speak Spanish when she's around. And she brings candles and pictures of saints with her, and she's always either praying or talking to dead relatives."

"Dead relatives?" Justine asked. She was looking at me strangely. In fact, they were all looking at me strangely. "Roni, your grandmother talks to dead people?"

Chapter 2

What a dumb thing to say, I thought miserably. *Now my friends are going to think my whole family is nuts.*

Just because my *abuela* chatted with her dead sister Rosa sometimes didn't mean she was totally screwy. In the old country it wasn't considered so strange to talk to spirits. But here it sounded pretty odd.

"She claims she visits with spirits," I explained haltingly.

"You mean she has psychic powers?" Justine asked excitedly.

"Sort of," I said.

"Neat," Karen added.

Justine and Karen looked really interested. I couldn't believe it. They didn't think it was weird. They were actually impressed!

"Maybe it runs in your family," Justine went on. "It often does. Have you ever talked to spirits?"

"Not exactly," I said.

"But you might have psychic energy waiting to be tapped," Karen said.

Ginger laughed. "She does have psychic energy," she said. "Remember that time you made the tablecloth levitate?"

"She did?" Justine asked.

"Shut up," I said. I remembered the time very well.

Ginger kept talking. "It was very impressive," she said. "Roni got up from the table, but her belt buckle was caught in the fringe of the tablecloth. So as she walked away, everything came flying off—tablecloth, food, china, silverware, and all."

The three of them burst out laughing. I felt pretty stupid. I was also mad at Ginger. Just because she'd known me for ten years didn't mean she had to tell everyone about all the dumb things I'd ever done!

"Actually, I'm pretty sure I do have certain powers," I said grandly, to cover my embarrassment.

"Really?" Karen asked.

The laughter left their faces.

"Several times I've dreamed something that actually happened. One time I dreamed the house next door caught fire, and it did a week later," I said. This was true. "My mother said that all the

21

women in our family have psychic ability." This wasn't.

"If you ever feel psychic," Justine said, "you can ask your spirit friends for the answers to the next math test. I got a *D* on the last one and my dad flipped his lid."

"If I decide to use my psychic powers," I said, "I won't waste them on stuff like math tests. I'll channel them to conjure up the perfect guy for myself."

"Hey, good idea," Karen said. "Conjure up one for me while you're at it!"

"If mine works, then I'll do the same for you," I said generously.

"How do you do this spirit connection?" Justine asked. "I played with a Ouija board once. It was scary."

"Did your head spin around?" Ginger asked her.

"I don't use Ouija boards," I cut in. "I just concentrate hard and make things materialize."

"Yeah, right," Ginger said. "When did you ever make something materialize?"

"You want me to show you?" I said. I was still mad at her. "I'll demonstrate right now, if you want. Get those candles."

"You want me to light Frosty the Snowman and Santa?" Ginger asked in horror.

"What's the point of candles if you never light them?"

"Okay, I guess," she said. She lit them. I turned off the light, and a pinkish glow lit the room.

I had no idea what I was doing, but the others seemed impressed, so I went on. I'd show Ginger who had the psychic powers around here! I put one of Ginger's scarves over my head and waved my arms over the candles.

"Oh, spirits of the great unknown, if you're out there, send me a sign," I chanted. Outside the wind tapped a branch against the window, and we all jumped. This was going great.

Even more enthusiastic now, I closed my eyes and waved my arms around some more. "Oh, spirits of the unseen world, send me the perfect guy," I sang. I frowned as I heard the others giggling. Then I stiffened and pointed dramatically at the wall. "I can see him!" I whispered.

"You can?" They weren't giggling now.

"Yes. He's gorgeous! Bright blue eyes, and long eyelashes, and dark brown hair, and a great smile, and muscles . . ."

"That's Tom Cruise," Ginger said. "You're looking at the poster on my wall."

"No, I'm not. I actually see this guy. I summoned him up for myself. I get the feeling that I'm going to be meeting him very soon . . . in the next few days."

"Wow," Justine said. They were all looking at me as if they weren't sure whether to believe me or not. I wasn't sure whether to believe me or not, either. I had been fooling around in the beginning, but now

I'd almost convinced myself that I did see a shape in the shadows. Ginger's robe hanging on the door really looked like someone was standing there—a tall, dark-haired guy. And suddenly he moved. I guess the robe must have stirred in a draft—it *was* pretty windy that night. But I leaped up, almost knocking over one of the candles.

"Quick, turn on the light!" I yelled.

Instantly the room was bathed in safe, warm light. The others were looking at me with terrified faces. "I thought someone was standing there," I said. "It got too creepy."

"It sure did," Karen agreed.

We tried to laugh about it. We ate all the brownies, but we still found it hard to relax. We kept looking at the shadows in the corner.

"I wish we were at my house," Justine said. "What we need right now is a soak in the hot tub."

"I've never been in a hot tub," Karen said.

"Never?" Justine sounded as horrified as if Karen had just said she'd never taken a shower. "Karen, you have to come over and try it. It's wonderful."

"It really is great, Karen," Ginger agreed. "We stayed at a hotel with a spa on our vacation last year. I loved being outdoors at night, sitting in hot bubbly water and looking up at the stars."

"Sounds wonderful," Karen said.

"Our hot tub is outside," said Justine. "Maybe we

24

could sleep over at my house next weekend . . ."

"Especially if your parents will be away again," Ginger added.

"Yeah, I'm kind of nervous about staying with your stepmother after all the things you've told us," Karen said.

"It's okay," Justine said. "She can be really nice to other people. Maybe I'll ask if I can have you all over."

"I'd like to have you all sleep over sometime, too," Karen said. "I want my folks to see how nice my friends are."

"They wouldn't think we were so nice if they'd seen us throwing popcorn before," I said. "But I want to see your house, too."

"And I'd like to meet your little sisters and brother," Karen said to me. "We could take turns."

"Good idea. Let's do it," Justine said.

"Roni will probably be too busy with the guy she just created with the help of her spirit friends to have time for sleepovers," Ginger said, nudging me.

"Shut up," I said. "I don't know about you guys, but I'm going to sleep. It's really hard work, talking to the spirit world."

I curled up in my sleeping bag. The room became quiet.

"I wish you hadn't brought up the spirit world again," Karen said through the silence. "I keep expecting that robe on the door to move."

Ginger got up and took down the robe. "Now can we all settle down?" she said. "I've known Roni since she was four years old and she's never been able to talk to spirits before. I don't see why she should start now. So let's all go to sleep, okay?"

"Okay," came Justine's muffled reply from her bag.

But I couldn't get to sleep. I was too excited. Had I really conjured up the guy of my dreams?

3

I walked home from Ginger's house the next morning, taking the short cut across the field. In the distance I could see the sun glinting on the skyscrapers of downtown Phoenix, with Camelback Mountain crouching behind them. There were dark lines of mountains on the horizon, but our area was completely flat. Until recently it had been a small agricultural community, but the city had gradually sprawled outward, and now there were more homes than fields. The cotton field between Ginger's house and mine was one of the few left, but there were still enough horses and chickens and corn growing in backyards to give the place a rural feel.

Most of the houses were pretty ordinary, ranch-style homes, very different from the mini-palaces going up in the new developments nearby. These were really changing the flavor of our community. Until now it had been mainly Mexican-American families, and most people worked on the land, except for people like my dad, who worked for the city. But now city people were moving into the new developments. Some of the homes in Regency Estates, the newest neighborhood in our area, looked like something out of a movie set, with their pillars and turrets and gazebos.

Our house definitely wasn't like that. It was one of the old ranch homes, on a big sprawling lot, where my father grew tomatoes and chili peppers and my mother kept a few hens. My bedroom was at the back of the house, looking out across the fields.

But when I got home that morning, I found that my bedroom wasn't my bedroom anymore. My bed had been pushed against the wall and my horse collection was gone from the top of my dresser.

"Wait a minute!" I yelled. "What's going on?"

My mother's head appeared around the door. She had a stack of sheets in her arms. "Oh, good, Roni, you're back," she said, dropping them onto the bed. "I need your help with this. Papa's already gone to the airport to meet Abuela."

"You're putting her in my room?" I demanded.

"What's wrong with Paco's room? That's where she usually sleeps."

"He's been waking up at night so much recently, I decided it was better to leave him be," my mother said. "I didn't want him to disturb your sisters."

"What about disturbing me? Where am I supposed to sleep?" I was grouchy from lack of sleep, and not ready to give an inch. After all, I was the oldest child in the family. I sure got all the responsibilities—some privileges had to come with the turf.

My mother looked up, clearly annoyed at my tone of voice. "In the henhouse, where else?" she said. Then she smiled. "We'll squeeze a cot in Carmen and Monica's room."

"I have to sleep on a cot?" I complained. "It's going to be hard and lumpy—I won't get any sleep at all."

"It's only for a little while," Mama said. "Anyone would think you weren't glad to see your *abuelita*, Roni."

Actually, I wasn't very glad, but I couldn't say that. "It's different now," I mumbled. "I'm in high school. I might want to have my friends over . . ."

"You're very welcome to have your friends over whenever you want," Mama said. "You know that. We'd like to meet your new friends, and we want you to fit in at high school. Invite them anytime. I'm sure Abuela will want to meet them, too."

"Oh, sure," I said. "Since they can't speak Spanish

29

and she can't speak English, they won't have too much to talk about. And since I'll have no place to entertain them, I'll be the only one who can't have her friends sleep over."

I scowled at my mother, to let her know how much she was messing up my life. She shrugged. "They can sleep over. I'll put down mattresses in the family room."

I winced. I knew I was being a jerk, while my mother was trying hard to be nice. But now that I thought about it, there was no way that I wanted my friends to come to my house anyway, at least not for the month my grandmother would be visiting. Our house just didn't look like a normal American house should. Justine's house didn't have pictures of saints on the walls, or a statue in the corner with rosaries hung on it. And Karen and Justine were both the only children in their families. They'd probably freak out here with hundreds of little brothers and sisters to bug them. (Well, three seems like hundreds. I've been told that I exaggerate a little.) Ginger knew what my house was like, but Karen and Justine were used to houses that looked like furniture store advertisements, with nothing out of place and no noisy kids or weird grandmothers in them.

"You finish making this bed, because I've got to get started on the tortillas," my mother commanded.

"The tortillas?" I asked in surprise. "We've got some in the freezer."

Mama put her finger to her lips. "Do you know what Abuela would say if she knew we ate store-bought tortillas?" she asked. "She'd think I was the world's worst housekeeper! She'd say I was letting my family starve."

"Do people make their own tortillas where she comes from?"

"Every day. Every meal."

"What a drag! All that time and energy."

Mama nodded. "I'm sure they taste better, but as you say, who has the time? I'd better get started on them so they're ready when your *abuela* gets here." She made a face. "I hope they turn out okay. I'm a little out of practice."

She gave me a wink and I smiled back. I was surprised that my mother still worried about pleasing her mother. But family was the most important thing to my parents. They loved to have visits from relatives. They would always get down the guitar and sing. Even Karen's family wasn't that bizarre, I was sure.

I was so busy all day, making sure that the house looked perfect for Abuela's arrival and that Monica, Carmen, and Paco looked like angels to meet her, that I didn't have any time to think about my impressive performance with the spirit world last night. I didn't think about it again until Abuela was installed in my father's armchair, which none of us were allowed to sit in, recounting everything that had happened in her town since we last saw her.

"You wouldn't recognize what they've done with the old market," she was saying in Spanish. "All glass and concrete—so ugly and noisy. I told my sister Rosa that she'd weep if she saw what was happening in the name of progress."

I drew my mother aside. "Is it true that Abuela talks to the spirit of her dead sister? I mean, is it possible that our family really does have psychic powers?" I asked.

Mama smiled and shook her head. "Abuela doesn't really believe that she talks to Aunt Rosa. It's just her way. We're as normal as the next family."

"Oh," I said, kind of disappointed. At least being queen of the psychics had given me some sort of status with my friends.

"Veronica? Where is Veronica?" I heard my grandmother's voice calling me in Spanish.

"Roni, your *abuela* wants you," my father called. "She's brought you a present."

"Look, Roni," Paco said. "Abuela brought me a present, too." He held up a brightly painted wooden truck.

"That's nice," I said.

"And she brought us presents," Carmen said, waving a woven hair barrette while Monica proudly displayed her new silver mirror.

"And this is for you, my oldest grandchild, *mi hija*," Abuela said, handing me a package with her wrinkled old hands. I opened the paper. Inside was a blouse. It was made mostly of white lace, with flowers and birds embroidered around the neck. It was very beautiful, but it was also the sort of thing you'd see at a Mexican folk festival.

"It's beautiful, Abuelita," I said, giving her a dutiful kiss on the cheek.

"You can wear it to school tomorrow," Mama said, beaming at me.

"Excuse me?" I said in English. "There is no way I'm wearing this to school."

"What's she saying?" Abuela asked in Spanish.

"She says it's too good to wear to school, Mama," my mother said. "She wants to save it for when she goes to a party."

Abuela's face lit up. "Ah, yes, a party, where she will dance with young men," she said. "I hope they have chaperons at your parties here, Roni."

"Don't worry," I muttered to myself in English. "If I'm wearing that blouse, nobody would want to dance with me anyway!"

The next morning I rode the bus to school with Ginger, glad to be back in my normal high school world again. One evening of family togetherness, plus a night with a sister who talks in her sleep, had been enough.

"So how was the Pop Warner football game?" I asked Ginger.

"Great," she said. "Well, more than great."

"You ran out and scored a touchdown for Ben's team?"

"Better than that," Ginger said. "One of the kids on his team asked Ben if I was his girlfriend."

"And?"

"And he got all shy about it—he actually blushed—and he said, 'Sort of.'"

"What do you mean, sort of?" I demanded. "He should have had the guts to come right out and say it, the creep."

Ginger smiled. "Not in front of hundreds of little kids, Roni. You know what they're like. I thought it was great of him to admit anything. And he did hold my hand on the way back to the car."

I glanced across at her as the bus went around a corner. She looked different, somehow. She had this dreamy, faraway look on her face, and she sort of glowed inside. "That's great, Ginger," I said. But I couldn't help feeling a stab of jealousy. Ginger was my best friend, and I was glad she'd gotten together with Ben. But I felt left out. I wanted some guy to blush about me one day. I wanted to have

34

the same silly, dreamy look on my face that Ginger had when she talked about Ben.

"You should have been there," Ginger was saying. "Plenty of high school football players came and we all hung around and talked after the game."

"I was otherwise occupied," I said bitterly.

"Oh, that's right. How's your grandmother?"

"She's the same as ever. Never stops talking, and she asks all sorts of embarrassing questions."

"To you or the spirits?"

I don't know why Ginger was bugging me lately. Usually we kidded each other all the time and it didn't bother me. But today I was annoyed. It seemed like Ginger was making fun of my grandmother. I laughed about Abuela talking to spirits, but I didn't want anyone else to.

"My mother says she doesn't really talk to her dead sister. It's just the way she puts things."

"Oh, so she doesn't have psychic powers after all," Ginger said. "In which case, you don't, either. I knew you were faking it on Saturday."

"I didn't say anything about psychic powers," I snapped. "I just said my grandmother doesn't talk to her sister. And if you want to know, I really did see something that night."

"Yeah, right," Ginger said. "You don't have to impress me, Roni. I've known you all your life."

"No kidding!" I said. "And you obviously can't wait

to blab about every embarrassing thing I've ever done."

"What's that supposed to mean?" Ginger looked surprised.

"Telling Karen and Justine about that time I pulled off the tablecloth."

"Roni, that was funny."

"To you it was. But I don't like being embarrassed. I already feel dorky enough."

Ginger turned to stare at me. "What are you talking about, Roni? You're one of the most confident people I've ever met. You never let anybody put you down."

"Not anymore," I said.

"Why not?"

"I guess I feel like a fish out of water at our new school," I confessed.

"But Roni, you were the one who was going to take Alta Mesa by storm. You said you were going to go up to all the cute boys and introduce yourself as Roney with a *y*, just to be more exciting."

"It didn't work out like that," I said with a sigh. "I had big hopes for this school. But now that I'm here, I feel really insecure."

"Why?" Ginger asked. "We know our way around now. The teachers are okay. The other kids are nice enough. And we have Karen and Justine."

"I guess it's because I'm different," I said. "My family isn't like anyone else's."

36

"You mean you're really from Mars?" she quipped. "Come on, Roni. You have nice parents, two cute little sisters, and a brother. You live in a house. You eat food. How are you different?"

"Enough ways to make me feel like an outsider," I said. "Maybe you haven't noticed, but this school is almost totally Anglo and snobby. I feel weird, Ginger. I'm not used to looking like an outsider."

"You don't look like an outsider. You look like a perfectly normal person," Ginger said.

"Oh, yeah? What about the skirt thing? No one else but Karen has to dress like that. And you want to hear worse? My *abuela* brought me a blouse. It's all lacy and embroidered, Ginger. Apparently it's traditional embroidery from our town. And you know what my mother said? She said, 'How nice. You can wear it to school tomorrow.' I nearly died."

"You're not wearing it," Ginger observed.

"Only because I convinced them I'd spoil it at school. Now they think I'm going to wear it to the next party I'm invited to. Ginger, what am I going to do? I feel like I've been zapped into a Mexican twilight zone."

Ginger was grinning.

"It's not funny," I said.

"I think you're making too much of little things," Ginger said. "You did just fine at our old school. You were a leader. You were funny. People liked

37

you. There's no reason why that should change. I agree we don't know too many people yet, but it's getting better."

"It's okay for you," I said. "You look like you belong. You've got your brother and Ben to look out for you. The only guys who have noticed my existence so far are the nerds. Is that the best I can do?"

Ginger patted my arm. "You really are down on yourself today, aren't you?"

"Not enough sleep two nights in a row, I guess," I said. "Don't worry, I'll snap out of it. I'll be back to my old cheerful self before you know—Holy cow! Look at that!"

"What?" Ginger leaned across to peer out the bus window with me.

"Look at that red convertible! It's turning into the school parking lot." I jumped up. "Quick, let's get off the bus. I have to see who drives a car like that. I only saw the back of his head, but it looked cute!" I started fighting my way down the aisle.

Ginger followed, laughing. "You weren't kidding when you said you were going to snap out of it! I knew it was impossible to keep you down for long."

We sprinted across the street, which isn't easy when the temperature is a hundred degrees. But by the time we got to the parking lot, the red convertible was already parked. There was no sign of its driver.

"Rats," I said. "I have to meet him, Ginger. I'd love

to drive around in a car like that. I bet he'd like a girl-friend named Roney with a *y*."

"He's probably a senior who wouldn't look twice at a little freshman," Ginger said.

"Not even a freshman called Roney with a *y*?" I asked hopefully.

Ginger rolled her eyes and led the way into the building. I was already feeling much better. My family seemed like a distant memory out in Oak Creek, and high school was full of possibilities.

We reached our lockers a minute or so before the bell for first period. I have the upper locker, Ginger the lower one. I had just started to open mine when I remembered that we had been in a hurry to catch our bus on Friday afternoon. I had crammed everything in and slammed the door shut on it.

Unfortunately I remembered this one fraction of a second too late. As I opened the locker a great cascade of books, papers, pencils, and rulers came shooting out.

"Whoa!" I exclaimed. I tried to shut the door on them, but it was too late. I jumped to safety.

A guy who was passing wasn't so lucky. He was suddenly deluged with a mountain of objects. He put his hands to his head to defend himself from a flying French book, stepped on a loose sheet of paper, and fell down in the middle of the hall.

Ginger and I surveyed the scene in horror. The

final sheets of my loose-leaf notebook were fluttering to rest around him. Other students were already rushing to his aid.

"Drew, are you okay? What happened?" someone asked.

Shakily he got to his feet. "I'm not sure," he said. "One minute I was on my way to class. The next . . . avalanche . . ." He gazed around the crowd until his eyes settled on me. That was when I got my first good look at him. He had dark brown curly hair, the longest eyelashes I had ever seen, great muscles under a black tank top, and amazing blue eyes.

"I can't believe that all came from one locker," he commented. "So tell me. Are you licensed to spill?" This got a laugh from the crowd and made my face turn from pink to crimson. He smoothed his hair back into place and picked up his backpack.

"I'm . . . uh . . . really sorry," I stammered. "Are you okay?"

"I'll survive," he said. He turned to his friends. "Just remind me to stay out of this hall from now on. If I'm late to class, none of the teachers will ever believe I was attacked by a locker."

He moved away with his group, leaving me standing in the middle of my own personal disaster area.

Ginger got down on her hands and knees and

started picking things up. "Come on, Roni. We'll be late for class," she said.

I didn't move.

"Roni? Are you okay?" Ginger asked.

I pointed down the hall. "Ginger, it's him," I stammered. "It's the guy I conjured up in your room!"

Chapter

4

"Now do you believe me?" I demanded excitedly as I watched the boy's back disappear down the hall.

"Believe what?"

"That I have psychic powers," I said triumphantly. "I'm not kidding, Ginger. I saw an image of that actual guy in your room. I swear I'm not making it up."

Ginger laughed uneasily. "You probably noticed him around school and thought he was cute. Then, when you had to create an ideal guy, he immediately came to mind."

"I'm sure I never saw him before. Don't you think I'd remember someone who looks like that?" I said. "Boy, that magic works fast. I invent him on Saturday, and on Monday morning, bam!"

"Bam is right," Ginger said. "I don't think attacking him with textbooks counts as a romantic first encounter."

This brought me back to reality fast. "You're right," I said. "He must think I'm a total klutz. I'm doomed, Ginger!"

"I wouldn't say that," Ginger said. "You didn't actually kill him."

"Doomed forever!"

Ginger was grinning. "Maybe your magic went wrong," she said. "Maybe one of those books was supposed to hit him hard enough to knock him senseless. Then, when he opened his eyes, the first face he'd see would be yours . . ."

"Yeah!" I said, not realizing that she was making fun of me.

"And he'd lost his memory," Ginger went on, "and all power of reason, so that he'd fall hopelessly in love with you."

"Ha, ha," I said. "I'll have you know that a guy doesn't have to be completely out of his mind to fall in love with me. I know it wasn't a very good beginning for us, but fate has strange ways of bringing people together. I just have to make sure that he sees me being funny and cool the next time we run into each other."

"I hope that's a figure of speech," Ginger quipped. "You better not run into him again, or you might scare him off for good."

We stuffed the last paper back into my locker. "Come on, we're really late now," Ginger said, almost dragging me down the hall.

In math class, I told Karen and Justine all about my encounter with fate, and they promised to find out anything they could about the guy my spirits had conjured up. A girl named Hilary, who sat in front of me, listened to my description of him and said, "That sounds like Drew Howard. Terrific muscles? Great tan? Incredible eyes?"

I nodded.

"That's him."

"Tell me more," I whispered, but the math teacher was frowning in my direction. At the end of class Hilary was swept out the door with her friends, so I had to wait in suspense until lunchtime.

Karen, Ginger, Justine, and I all met under our favorite tree. It's really too hot to eat outside in Phoenix in late September, but we had found the cafeteria so loud and scary on the first day of school that we'd settled for a shady spot outside. Now we kind of liked it. It had become *our* spot, where we could sit and watch the world go by.

That afternoon, I was the last to arrive. Three pairs of eyes looked up at me expectantly.

"Boy, you don't do things halfway, do you?" Karen said as I sat down.

"Meaning what?"

"Meaning that you had to pick Drew Howard to maim with your flying books," Justine said bluntly.

"I didn't maim him. I just dazed him a little," I said. "So what did you find out about him? Hilary was about to tell me when Mr. Hudson made us shut up."

"What did we find out?" Justine said dramatically. "Only that he's the most popular sophomore there is: class president *and* star running back for the frosh-soph team."

"And he just happens to drive a red convertible," Ginger added, "like the one that made you freak out this morning."

"That was the good news," Karen said. "The bad news is that he's dating Charlene Davies. You know, perky blond cheerleader and Miss Popularity?"

"Next time you get the spirits to summon up a guy for you, have them send one within your reach," Ginger said.

"My spirits only do top-of-the-line creations," I said. "And I still think it was fate that brought us together. You know stuff falls out of my locker all the time. But I've never seen it come flying out like that before. It was like a poltergeist! I bet my spirits hit him with the books on purpose."

My three friends laughed at me.

"Frankly, Roni, I don't think you have a chance of getting him to notice you, spirits or not," Justine said.

"Maybe, just maybe, if you were used to sophisticated boys and wore more makeup . . ."

"If *only* I could be exactly like you, Justine," I said. But even Justine's opinions couldn't bother me today.

"Okay, listen up," I announced. "This is an assignment for the Boyfriend Club. Drew Howard has to see me as a desirable mystery woman and forget that I was ever a klutz."

"We're a boyfriend club, not a group of miracle workers," Ginger said with a snort.

"And he does already have a girlfriend," Justine reminded me.

That made me stop and think for a second. I've always thought that girls who stole other girls' boyfriends were only one step above pond scum. "Maybe they're getting tired of each other," I said hopefully. "Maybe they're about to break up anyway."

"Do you really think he'd dump Charlene for you?" Justine asked in that sweet, encouraging way of hers. "Dream on."

The truth was, I didn't think it could happen, but that's never stopped me before. "So? He's not going to go steady with her until he's seventy-five, is he? If you guys help me get him to notice me, I'll be next in line when they do break up."

"Of course we'll help," Karen said warmly. "It would be wonderful if you ever could get together with a guy like that, Roni, but I wouldn't hope for too much."

"All I need to do is to erase that horrible first impression," I said thoughtfully. "The only thing Drew knows is that I was standing there with my mouth open while my books knocked him down. The next time he sees me, he's got to think I'm cool and interesting and incredibly beautiful. How are we going to do that?"

"Short of a complete makeover, I couldn't say," Justine answered.

"Shut up, Justine," Karen said. "Let's start some positive thinking around here. The first thing you could try is changing the way you look."

Justine opened her book bag. "We'll start with your makeup," she said.

"I don't really wear makeup," I told her. I didn't mention that my mother had threatened to scrub my face if she ever saw me with lipstick on.

"Exactly," Justine said smugly. "And no guy is going to notice you unless you highlight your best features." She took out a large cosmetic bag and tipped a bunch of lipsticks, mascara wands, and every other kind of beauty aid onto the grass. "There should be something here that you could use."

"What did you do, rob a makeup store?" Ginger asked.

"Most of this stuff is my stepmother's," Justine said. "Like I said before, she buys so much, she doesn't notice if I borrow anything."

I felt a little uneasy as Justine took her stepmother's eyeliner and painted a thin brown line around my eye, followed by a few swipes of her stepmother's mascara. I didn't really want to be part of the makeup-stealing plot. If Justine's stepmother was half as bad as Justine said she was, I'd rather not get on her bad side!

"Justine, are you sure you should be using this stuff on me?" I asked.

"Just be quiet and hold still," she said. "I've got a great lipstick here—Charles of the Ritz, Strawberry Parfait. Perfect. You should always wear red. You have the coloring for it."

She finished my lips. "There," she said. "You look better already."

"She's right, Roni," Karen said. "You look really glamorous."

I stood up. "I'd like to thank all the little people," I began, posing like a movie star. "And as for the rumor that there's something between me and a certain gorgeous guy—"

"Hi, Roni!" called a squeaky voice. It was the type of voice that gets on your nerves instantly. It belonged to Owen, the shrimpiest, skinniest guy in school and the leader of the nerd pack. Before we knew what was happening, we were surrounded by nerds.

"Hi, girls," Ronald said.

"Hi," Wolfgang mumbled.

Walter just stood there and grinned.

It was a horrible sight, the four of them squinting hopefully at us, hair sticking up every which way, pants a foot too short, Wolfgang in his perennial purple-and-brown stag sweater. Justine couldn't get her makeup back into the bag fast enough. The others were already looking for escape routes.

"If I may say so," Ronald went on, leering at me in his repulsive manner, "you're looking very lovely today, Roni. I don't suppose you'd like to go to a movie tonight? They're showing *Creature from the Black Lagoon,* and that's one of my favorites."

My friends were just standing there, smirking, as I made "get me out of here" signs over Owen's head.

"Oh, no, is that the art building on fire?" I asked. But before I could get any nerds to react to this, I saw a group of kids coming down the path toward us. They were laughing loudly, and they walked like they owned the place. These kids were obviously the "in" crowd, kids who mattered. And right in the middle of the group was Drew Howard. He had his arm around a really pretty girl, presumably Charlene. My heart did a flip-flop. He had the most adorable smile!

He must have felt me staring at him, because he suddenly looked in my direction. I saw his expression change when he remembered who I was. Then he must have said something to his friends, because they all turned to stare at me. There I was, surrounded by my nerdy fan club, praying that one of my spirit friends would hear my wish and zap me out of there. But the spirits must have been out to lunch, because I saw Charlene look back at me, nudge the girl next to her, and giggle. Now I really was forever doomed. In Drew's eyes I was no longer just a klutz. I was also a nerd groupie.

Chapter 5

"Everyone has bad days sometimes, Roni," Ginger said on the way home. "Don't let it upset you. I'm sure tomorrow will be just fine."

"I don't think anything will be just fine ever again," I said with a big sigh. "I've blown it completely with Drew."

Ginger looked at me sympathetically. "I know how you feel, Roni," she said gently. "But let's face it, you never did have much of a chance with him. He's out of your league, don't you think?"

"I guess," I admitted.

"I mean, popular football players are hardly likely to notice new little freshman girls—"

"Okay, okay! You've made your point!"

"I was going to add, however attractive and funny."

I smiled at her. "Thanks, but I don't feel attractive and funny right now. I feel stupid. You're right—how could I ever compete with Miss All-American Cheerleader Charlene? Even though I'm sure I'm much more fun to be with," I added.

"Maybe there could be a Drew in your future," Ginger suggested. "By the time you're a junior and he's a senior, you could be popular, too."

"Yeah, and pigs could start flying," I said.

She gave me a dig in the ribs. "Come on. It could happen. You just have to start low and work your way up to Drew."

"You're not suggesting I date a nerd?"

"Not that low," she said. "I was suggesting you find a nice ordinary guy . . ."

"Like Ben?"

"Like Ben," she agreed with a smug smile. "Although I guess your guy probably wouldn't be as cute as Ben."

"Has anyone told you you've become totally sickening?" I asked.

She grinned. "Okay, maybe you can find someone *almost* as cute as Ben—and as nice. Nice is important. Lots of those popular guys are total jerks."

"I'm sure Drew wouldn't be a total jerk," I said wistfully.

"Get Drew out of your mind right now," she instructed. "Think positive. Decide that you are going to find yourself a normal, friendly, obtainable boyfriend. Start planning how the Boyfriend Club can help you meet a guy like that. Go through the student handbook tonight and figure out which club is a likely place to meet guys. Make a positive plan. Then you'll feel better."

"Okay," I said. "I suppose you're right. I was being very immature today. I've got to forget about Drew and get on with my life."

"There you go," Ginger said. "We'll check out all the clubs tomorrow. Maybe we'll even find a fun new thing to do."

I went home and leafed through the school handbook. Not many clubs met at lunchtime, but I circled a few. The video club sounded okay. I wouldn't mind starring in my own movie. And the radio club could be interesting—who wouldn't want to hear me on their radio? I decided to check them all out this week, one after the other. Anything rather than go through the embarrassment I'd suffered at lunch today. I could still see Charlene's face as she laughed at me.

I lay back on my bed with a sigh. I'd had such high hopes for Alta Mesa High. I'd been sure that this school would be a million times better than our crummy school out at Oak Creek, where we'd known all the boys since kindergarten, and their only interests were pickup trucks and sports. Ginger and I had talked about meeting exciting guys who knew there was more to life than football. We'd dreamed of being instantly popular and successful, making hundreds of new friends.

Instead of that, my image had been ruined in a few short weeks. I was now Roni, the hick who showed up for her first day of high school in a long skirt. Roni, whose family wanted her to wear a frilly lace blouse to parties. And worst of all, I was now Roni the klutzy nerdette. It couldn't get much worse, could it?

Yes, it could. And it did, immediately. As I took out my binder to do my homework, I noticed unfamiliar writing on a piece of paper. The writing was in French and the name at the top of the paper was Andrew Howard.

My heart did a quick flip. It took me a second to realize that it was Drew's paper. What was Drew's paper doing in my binder? For one crazy moment I thought he must have put it there so we'd have an excuse to meet again.

Right, Roni! Get real, I told myself. If Drew Howard wanted a girl, he wouldn't have to hide French papers in her notebook. He'd snap his fingers and she'd come running—at least, I would. I began to go hot all over as I realized what must have happened. Drew must have dropped his paper when I knocked him down with my flying library. And I'd scooped it up with my papers and stuffed it into my binder. Now he was going to be mad at me again!

Then a more hopeful thought crossed my mind. Maybe, just maybe, he hadn't even missed it . . . which gave me a wonderful opportunity to make up for my klutziness! Tomorrow I'd bring him the paper and say, "Here, Drew, I found this!" And he'd say, "Thanks, Roni, you saved my life. I'd have gotten an *F* if I hadn't turned that in." And then he'd smile at me with that wonderful smile of his.

The next day I looked for Drew everywhere, but I didn't see him all morning. Ginger and I tried out the video club at lunchtime. Karen had been checking out the handbook, too, and thought she might meet intelligent guys at the chess club. Ginger and I were sure that romantic moments were not likely to happen while a guy was jumping over our pawns with his knight, but Karen said you never know. Justine had to go to the library to write an English essay.

"Maybe an incredibly cute guy will be sitting at the next table, all alone in that big, empty library," she said. "Our eyes will meet and he'll whisper—"

"'Can I borrow your pen?'" Karen teased.

Justine made a face at her, and we all headed off in our various directions. The video club met in a special projection room at the back of the little theater. It was dark as Ginger opened the door. We stood nervously in the entrance, not sure anyone was inside. But suddenly a voice came out of the darkness—a very squeaky voice. "Don't just stand there; close the door. We can't see the screen."

Ginger and I leaped back simultaneously, letting the door slam shut again. We stood outside in the bright sunlight, breathing hard, staring at each other in horror.

"Tell me I'm wrong. I thought that was Ronald's voice I heard in there," I said as soon as I could breathe again.

Ginger nodded. "Sounded awfully like it."

"Thank goodness he didn't see who we were. Thank goodness we got out in time," I said.

Ginger shuddered. "Can you imagine being trapped in a dark video room with Ronald and the other nerds?"

"It's too horrible to think about," I said. "Let's get away from here before nerds start creeping out to drag us inside."

We ran.

"So how was the video club?" Karen called as she came down the hall to meet us at the end of lunch hour.

"You don't want to know," I said. "We're never going back there again."

56

"How come?"

"Let's just say that my idea of bliss isn't being stuck in a dark projection room with Ronald and who knows how many invisible nerds."

Karen shuddered.

"How was the chess club?" Ginger asked.

"A little too serious for me," Karen said. "I played against one guy who spent twenty minutes explaining why my first move was a mistake. We didn't get any further than that."

"No cute guys?"

"Not even close."

"Forget the chess club, then," I said. "This is getting depressing. Where do all the cute guys go at lunchtime? Do you think there's a secret hideout somewhere?"

"Check the list for a cute guy club," Ginger suggested.

"Just find out where Drew Howard eats his lunch," Karen said. "I bet all the other cute guys will be there, too."

"Now that's not a bad idea," I said.

"I thought you wanted to stay away from Drew until he'd forgotten about your little incident," Ginger said.

"I did, but now I have a way of getting back into instant favor with him," I told her triumphantly.

"What?" Ginger demanded.

"I happen to have found his missing French paper," I said. "He'll be eternally grateful when I give it back to him. *And* it will be the perfect way to start a conversation."

I didn't mention that the missing paper had shown up in my binder, or that I was responsible for it getting lost in the first place.

"Okay, let's go look for him," Karen said, dragging me to my feet.

By the end of lunch hour we decided that there really must be a secret hideout for popular guys. There definitely weren't any hanging around the campus. When the bell rang for afternoon classes, we were no closer to discovering Drew's secret hideout.

But as I arrived at my French room, Drew was on his way out. We nearly collided in the doorway. He didn't look very happy, but I took a chance and waved the paper at him.

"Oh, Drew, I've been looking for you to give you this," I said. "You lost it and I found it."

He looked at the paper and then at me. "You again!" he said, grabbing the paper from my hand. "So that's where it was. I knew I had it with my stuff yesterday morning. I must have dropped it when I got knocked senseless by your books."

"It got mixed up with my stuff," I said. "I thought you'd be glad to have it back."

He looked at me coldly. "You're a little too late," he said. "Tell me, have you been sent here on a specific mission to destroy my life?"

"I'm sorry about the locker," I mumbled. "It was an accident. It could have happened to anyone."

"Yeah, but what about my homework?" he demanded. "Madame gave me after-school detention for three days because I didn't turn it in. Strangely enough, she wouldn't buy my story about being hit by unidentified flying objects in the hall."

He was still glaring at me. I felt my face turning beet red.

"I'm . . . uh . . . really sorry," I stammered. "Do you want me to turn it in to Madame now and tell her it was my fault?"

"It won't do any good," he said. "She's got it in for me because I've been making people laugh in her class. And I've already missed a couple of assignments this year, so she's not willing to forgive and forget anymore."

"I feel terrible," I said.

"Not as bad as I do. The coach almost killed me when I showed up late to practice yesterday because of this detention—and I'll be late for two more days."

"Is there anything I can do?"

"Just stay away from me," he said. He looked at his watch. "Oh, great. Now I'm going to be late to math, and that teacher has it in for me, too."

He ran off down the hall. I slunk into French. I don't think I'd ever felt worse in my life.

On the way home I told Ginger what had happened. She laughed. "I'm sorry, Roni. I know what you must be going through," she said. "But when you look back on this, you'll think it was funny."

"When I look back on it, I'll be living in a monastery in Tibet," I said. "I'm never showing my face around here again. Can you imagine how Miss Perfect Charlene is going to laugh about me now?"

"Who cares what a snob like Charlene thinks?" Ginger demanded. "She doesn't rule the universe. The old Roni Ruiz would never have cared what a stuck-up cheerleader thought about her. Remember how we used to make fun of the cheerleaders at our old school and how stupid they looked kicking their legs over their heads?"

"That was only because we couldn't do it," I said. "We were jealous." It occurred to me that I was still jealous. Not only was Charlene a good cheerleader, but she had Drew, too. Even more than that, she made me feel worthless, and I hated to feel that way.

"Things will be better tomorrow," Ginger said. "You'll see."

The next day I refused to eat under the tree. "I don't care how crowded the cafeteria is; I'm not eating outside anymore," I said. "I don't want to risk Drew and his friends seeing me. I'm going to be totally invisible from now on. I'm thinking of changing religions and wearing one of those veils that covers everything except my eyes."

My friends laughed. They didn't seem to realize how serious I was. They saw everything that had happened so far as a minor embarrassment, not the end of the world. But they came inside with me anyway.

The cafeteria was just as overwhelming as it had been on the first day of school: noise bouncing off the tiled walls, the whir of the air conditioner forcing everyone to yell over it, and the usual screams, laughs, and clatter of plates. If seemed as if all three thousand students were crammed in here at once. We stood in the doorway, holding our lunch bags and feeling like goldfish who had stumbled on sharks in a feeding frenzy.

Then I saw it: an empty table in the far corner.

"I'll get it!" I yelled. I sprinted across the room, dodging students, tables, benches, and garbage cans. I'd gotten about halfway to the other side of the cafeteria when I realized that my friends weren't with me. They must not have noticed the table when I did. I looked over my shoulder, waving frantically in their direction. "You guys!" I screamed. "There's a table in the corner."

As I turned back, I was conscious of a shape looming up in front of me. There was nothing I could do. The person and I collided. At least, his tray and I collided. I won. The tray and its contents went flying.

It all seemed to happen in slow motion, another nightmare scene from which there was no escape. When it was over, I wasn't at all surprised to find that the person I had collided with was Drew, and that he now had an interesting brownish red stain down the front of his white shirt.

"Oh, no," he wailed. "I don't believe it. Not again!"

Before I could do anything sensible, like get out of there, someone else appeared on the scene. Charlene froze when she saw the stain on Drew's shirt.

"What happened to your clothes?" she yelled.

"I decided to absorb my chili directly through my skin instead of going to the trouble of eating it," he said dryly. Charlene just looked confused, so Drew continued, "What do you think happened? Some idiot knocked my tray."

I tried to back away quietly, but Charlene's gaze had already zoomed in on me. "Her again?" she demanded. "Wasn't she the one who knocked you down in the hall?"

By this time, my friends had pushed their way through the crowd toward me.

"Look, it was an accident," Ginger said, stepping between me and Charlene. "They were both accidents—"

But she didn't get to finish. Charlene moved past Ginger. Her eyes started spitting fire in my direction. "What's the matter with you? Are you a total klutz?" she yelled. Her voice was loud enough so that anyone who wasn't already watching now turned in our direction. People seated far away even stood up to get a better view.

"I told you I was sorry," I said, trying to escape gracefully.

"Sorry's not good enough. His shirt is ruined!"

"What do you want me to do, take it to a Laundromat?" I demanded. I was so embarrassed now, I could feel tears stinging in my eyes.

"You want her to buy him a new one?" Justine snapped, her voice perfectly matching Charlene's snobby tone. "Here. I have money."

"Cool it, Charlene," Drew said. "It's no big deal."

"Just stay out of our way," Charlene hissed at me.

I could feel a hand on my arm. "Come on, Roni. Let's get out of here," came Karen's soothing voice. I allowed myself to be led away.

"What are we going to do about your shirt?" I heard Charlene say loudly.

"Wash it, I guess."

"I meant for tonight. Have you forgotten we're meeting my folks right after football practice?"

"Oh, yeah. Well, I have a T-shirt in my PE locker,"

Drew said. He looked like a naughty little boy being scolded by his mother.

"A T-shirt? You can't wear a PE shirt out to dinner with my folks," she snapped. "We'll have to stop at the mall and pick up a shirt on the way. See if you can get out early tonight."

"I don't think I can. I was late last night because of detention. . . ."

I didn't wait around to hear any more. I hurried away between my friends before Drew could mention that I was also the person responsible for that. *It's okay,* I decided. *I'll transfer back to Las Lomas High in Oak Creek. Pretty soon everyone at Alta Mesa will have forgotten that Roni Ruiz ever existed.*

When I got home, nobody was there except my grandmother, sitting in her favorite chair, quietly snoozing. She woke as I dropped my book bag onto the table.

"Ah, *mi hija,* how was your day at school?"

"Don't ask," I said. "Where's Mama?"

"She's taken the little ones to the store with her. What's wrong, child?"

"I wanted to ask Mama something," I said.

"You had a bad day at school?" Abuela asked, her face bright and alert now. "Come and sit next to your *abuela* and tell me about it."

"It wasn't just a bad day," I said. "It was about the

worst day of my life." I sank down onto the sofa. "I made such a fool of myself, Abuela."

"What did you do?"

"You wouldn't understand," I said.

She sat up and looked at me with surprisingly bright, clear eyes. "You think schools weren't invented in my generation?" she asked. "You think I was never a child? I was never embarrassed?"

When I didn't answer, she took my hand and started telling me a story. "When I was your age—maybe a little younger—my father died. My mother made me wear black to school for a year. I was a pale, skinny child. Can you imagine how I looked in a long black dress with my hair in a big black bow? The other children called me the Black Widow. Whenever they saw me, they would laugh and say, 'Watch out. Here comes the Black Widow. Make sure she doesn't bite you.'" She leaned forward in her chair. "It took me a while to realize that they could say what they liked, but they couldn't actually hurt me. I got over it, and so will you."

"My day was much worse than that," I said. "I can't go back there, Abuela. I'm going to ask Mama if I can transfer back to Las Lomas here in Oak Creek."

Abuela gazed at me so intensely with her piercing black eyes that I began to feel uncomfortable. "Is that how you were brought up?" she asked.

"What?"

"Running away when something gets too hard for you. That's not how your parents behaved. Your papa had a hard time when he first came to this country, and look at him now: a respected man in the community. If he'd run away, he'd still be working his father's fields in the old country."

"But it's different for grown-ups," I said. "They don't feel things like teenagers do."

Abuela snorted. "I suppose you think your generation invented teenagers, too," she said. "Everyone has gone through the same thing. We've all had times when we were so hurt and embarrassed we wanted to die. But I'll tell you one good thing about being a teenager."

"What?"

"Teenagers have short memories. If you do something stupid, everyone will forget within a week, because someone else will do something more stupid than you."

"You mean it?" I had to laugh.

"Of course. That's the way of things. It's not always easy to fit in right away. But soon you'll have forgotten that you were ever a newcomer and a stranger."

I got up and went to sit on the arm of her chair. "Do you really think so, Abuela?"

"I'm sure of it," she said. "And remember something else."

"What is that?"

"That you are one of the lucky ones . . . you have a family who loves you. You have a rock to cling to in stormy times."

I wrapped my arms around her frail body. "I'm really glad you came, Abuelita," I said.

Chapter 6

"What are you doing?" Justine asked.

I peered around the corner, scanning the entire hallway. "I'm waiting until it's safe to go to class," I said.

"What do you mean, safe?" Justine asked, looking at me as if I'd suddenly flipped. "Are there terrorists at Alta Mesa I don't know about?"

"I want to make sure that Drew and his friends are nowhere around," I said. "I don't want them to see me."

"Roni, you can't go through four years of high school avoiding Drew and his friends," Justine said. "For one thing, he has a lot of friends."

I sighed. It seemed like I was doomed. At home with my family, I had almost convinced myself that Abuela was right: everyone would soon forget how dumb I had been and I could get on with my life. But at school I was a nervous wreck. I thought of myself as Roni, the walking time bomb. I was terrified that I'd do some terrible damage every time I stepped outside the classroom. I looked up and down the hall again. So far, so good. It looked like Drew, Charlene, and the entire popular crowd had already gone to class. I took out my sunglasses and turned up my shirt collar.

Justine seemed amused. "Now you look like a spy," she said.

"I can't help it. I don't want anyone to recognize me," I said. "Oh, well, here goes nothing!"

I slunk out and hugged the edge of the hall, looking away as other students passed me. I had almost reached the end when Charlene and her friends came around the corner. There was nothing else to do: I dove into the nearest girls' bathroom. To my horror, the voices came closer. I had just managed to lock myself in a stall when Charlene came in, followed by two other cheerleaders.

"So what happened then?" one of the other girls was asking.

"My dad was really mad because we were late and we had reservations for six-thirty," Charlene said. "He couldn't believe I made Drew stop and buy a shirt. But I mean, I couldn't sit next to somebody wearing a PE shirt, could I?"

"Of course not. Was his other shirt ruined?"

"Totally."

"What bad luck."

"More than bad luck. It's that same girl. I don't know what's with her, but I think she's out to get Drew."

"Who is she?"

"I don't know. Some freshman creep."

At least she hadn't found out my name yet. That was one good thing. I waited for them to go, but they didn't seem as if they planned to leave anytime that day. Through the crack in the door I could see them putting on makeup and brushing their hair as they talked.

"So do you think your mom will let you go to the lake with Drew?"

"I'm not going to tell her who I'm going with, stupid," Charlene said. "She thinks I'm going with a group of girls."

"Good move. I wish I'd thought of that."

"Andrea, tell your mom you're sleeping over at my place."

"I'll think about it."

"I just hope we have the lake to ourselves this time," came Charlene's voice again, loud and clear. "Remember last time, when those creepy Mexican guys were there fishing?"

"Yeah, what nerve, right next to our beach."

70

"It seems like you can't go anywhere anymore—"

"Was that the bell?" one of the girls said. "I've still got to put up my hair. Oh, well, late again."

"No problem. It's Fisher. He doesn't care."

I heard their voices fade away as the bathroom door closed behind them. I felt sick inside from the way they'd talked about Mexicans. *Boy, are they out of line*, I thought. *They even think they own all the lakes around here!*

But I didn't have time to think about it, because I was majorly late! I left the bathroom and sprinted down the hall to my math class. I had Mr. Hudson, and he *did* care if anyone was late. In fact, he always took roll the moment the bell rang.

By the time I reached the classroom, he was in the middle of roll. If I was lucky, I could sneak to my place and he'd never notice.

"Jennifer Thomas? Ryan Thompson?"

Rats, I thought. He was already past the *R*'s. Could I bluff, and make him think that he had missed me by accident? I didn't want to be marked absent, because that would go down as a cut. When he finished, I raised my hand. "Excuse me, Mr. Hudson. I think you missed me," I said in my most humble voice. Most teachers are moved by humble. Mr. Hudson wasn't one of them.

His eyes fastened on me. "I didn't miss you. I called your name and you weren't here. What's more . . ." He

71

checked his little book. "You have two other tardies already this semester. Three tardies equal one detention."

"Detention? Me?"

"Would you rather I lowered your grade?"

"No, sir," I mumbled.

I couldn't believe it. I'd never had detention before. In middle school only real troublemakers got detention—you know, kids who were always fighting or were rude to teachers. My parents were going to freak out when they heard. They were very big on respect and discipline. They'd probably ground me until I was twenty-one, maybe even until I was forty-five. I'd have to make sure they never found out.

At the end of the period I grabbed Ginger. "You've got to help me," I begged. "Call my mom when you get home and come up with a good reason why I'm late. Tell her I had to study in the library or work on a special project or something. My mind's a blank right now."

"Okay. I'll think of something," she said. "Why were you late, anyway?"

"I got trapped in the bathroom by Charlene Davies."

Ginger grinned. "It hasn't been your week, has it?"

"You can say that again," I muttered. "Do you think the spirits are punishing me for what I did on Saturday night?"

"Roni!" Ginger said, shaking her head.

"Well, it makes sense, doesn't it? I mean, when I started that stuff with the candles, I was just fooling around. It was only in the middle I began to believe it. Maybe they're mad at me and they're paying me back."

"Roni, there are no spirits," Ginger said, grabbing my shoulders and shaking me.

"Then explain why all these terrible things keep happening to me."

"Everybody has bad weeks. Yours has been worse than most," Ginger said. "But it wasn't caused by any angry spirits."

"I'm not so sure," I said. "I'm going to talk to my grandmother about it."

Ginger put a friendly hand on my shoulder. "What you suffer from is an overactive imagination."

"I do not!"

"Oh, no? Who was the one who panicked our entire kindergarten class by yelling that there was a flying saucer in the playground?"

"That was a natural mistake. I'd never seen a Frisbee before."

"But you said you saw a lot of little green men getting out of it."

"I thought I did."

"There you are. Definitely an overactive imagination."

"Okay. Maybe it's a little bit overactive," I agreed. "I'll try to keep it in check. No more spirits. No more

73

dream guys. I'll be sane and sensible and stay out of trouble from now on."

Ginger laughed. "I'll believe it when I see it," she said.

Detention actually wasn't too bad. I got all my homework done, so I was feeling pretty pleased with myself as I came out of school and made my way to the bus stop. The school yard was deserted. Only a couple of cars remained in the parking lot, and no one was hanging around the front entrance. Cars sped past the lonely bus stop. *Okay,* I said to myself, *so I'm all alone in the middle of a big, scary city where people get mugged all the time. But I'm not going to panic. I can take care of myself. I'm cool.* I jumped when I heard a scream across the street. A little boy came running out of one of the condos, chased by a mean-looking woman. As she grabbed his arm, he yelled and fought. "No, let go of me!" he screamed. "I don't want to go. I won't go!"

The woman didn't listen to him. She half-dragged him over to a parked car and shoved him inside while I watched in horror. I'd seen kidnappings on TV, of course, but I never thought I'd actually witness one!

Then it hit me: I could do something to prevent this terrible crime. I couldn't get across the busy street, but I could call the police.

As I ran back through the parking lot, I saw someone getting into a car. The engine started as I drew closer.

"Hey, wait. I need your help!" I yelled. It was then that I noticed that the car was a red convertible, driven by Drew. I didn't stop to think about what had happened between me and Drew this week. A kid's life was in danger! That was more important than any of my embarrassing scenes. I wrenched open the door and jumped into the car beside him. He recoiled with horror when he saw who it was, but before he could say anything I blurted, "Quick, follow that Volvo! A woman has just kidnapped a child."

"Are you serious?" He didn't look as if he believed me.

"I saw it, I swear," I insisted. "She dragged the kid into the car and he was screaming for help."

"Then call the police."

"What if she hands him over to an accomplice before the police catch up with her and the accomplice drives the kid away in another car? Come on, Drew. You've got to help that poor little boy. This is your chance to be a hero."

"Okay," he said. "The Volvo, you say?" He swung into the street, tires screeching. We could see the Volvo ahead, moving quickly through the traffic. Drew pulled out and tried to catch up, but rush hour was beginning and the traffic was heavy. We got caught behind a bus, and it looked like we'd lost them. Then I spotted the Volvo turning off toward Tempe.

"Quick, make a right!" I screamed. Drew swung the car around the corner.

"Where did it go?" he yelled to me.

We almost passed the old brick building before I saw the Volvo parked in the driveway. At the top of a flight of steps a door was just swinging shut.

"You see, I was right," I said. "This is where they switch cars or change the child's appearance or something criminal like that."

"What do you think we should do?" Drew asked. He looked really excited now.

"There's a phone booth across the street. I'll call the police. You keep watching. Don't let them leave."

"Oh, great. How exactly am I going to prevent a car from leaving?" he asked.

"Park across the driveway."

"Then they might ram my car."

"Don't be so selfish. We're talking about a little boy's life," I said. It's funny, but everything that had happened between Drew and me had been blanked out of my memory. Right now I was the one in command. "Besides," I went on, "they wouldn't want to draw attention to themselves by ramming a car."

"I suppose not."

"They might shoot you, though."

"Thanks a lot. I'll call the police and they can shoot you."

"They're not going to shoot anybody," I snapped. "It's a busy street. Now swing around and park across the driveway."

I crossed the street. Out of the corner of my eye I watched Drew park so that he was blocking the entire exit. My hands were shaking as I picked up the phone. Did you need money to dial 911? I put it in anyway. A second later an impersonal voice said, "Emergency, how may I direct your call?"

"Give me the police," I said. "I want to report a crime in progress."

"And your name, please?"

"It doesn't matter about my name!" I yelled. "I've just seen a child kidnapped and shoved into a car! We've got them cornered, so get a police car out here quick!"

"Your exact location?" she asked.

"I'm on the corner of . . ." I tried to locate a street sign. As I looked around I saw that a woman in a pink uniform was talking to Drew. We'd been discovered. We had to get the police here, now! Why weren't street signs ever where they were supposed to be?

"Are you still there, miss?" the operator asked.

"Just a minute. I'm trying to find the street name."

Drew was coming across the street toward me.

The lady in pink was going back up the steps. What could he possibly have told her?

"Okay," I said to the dispatcher. "I've got it. It's the corner of—"

"Roni, could I talk to you please?" Drew said, tapping me on the shoulder.

"Let me give her the directions first so the police can get here," I hissed. "The corner of—"

"Roni, I don't think we need the police," he said, covering the mouthpiece firmly with his hand.

"Of course we need the police!"

He grabbed my arm. "No, we don't. That woman came out to tell me I was blocking the driveway and their patients couldn't get in or out."

"Patients? It's a clinic! They're going to drug him!"

"Actually, they're going to put a filling in his tooth," Drew said dryly. "It's a dentist's office, Roni. The little boy was freaking out because he hates going to the dentist."

"Huh! Good cover story."

"The woman is his mother. They have regular appointments at the office. So do his father and big sister."

"Oh," I said.

"Excuse me, miss. What was the street name?" the dispatcher asked impatiently.

"Sorry, wrong number," I said, slamming down the phone.

"Come on," Drew said, grabbing my arm. "Let's

get out of here before the police come looking for us."

We climbed into the car and Drew sped away.

"I'm glad I didn't give them my name," I said. I was feeling hot and clammy all over. "How was I supposed to know?" I demanded. "It looked like a kidnapping. She shoved him into the car, and he was screaming."

"Kids often scream when they have to go to the dentist. I used to," Drew replied.

"Okay," I said angrily. "But what if I'd been right? What if I'd seen a kidnapping and done nothing about it, and then heard on the news that a child was missing? How do you think I'd feel then?"

Drew looked at me for a minute, then nodded. "You're right," he said. "You might be a totally screwy person, but you've got guts. Most people wouldn't want to get involved."

"I'm sorry," I said in a small voice. His unexpected kindness was having a strange effect on me. I felt like I might cry at any second. "You probably think I'm the weirdest person you ever met. I'm not usually a walking disaster area. Being close to you just seems to have this effect on me."

He grinned. "Girls often say I have a strange effect on them, but luckily it doesn't turn most of them into screwballs."

"I'll leave you alone after this, I promise," I said. "I'll stop making your life miserable. I won't throw things at you or lose any more homework or take you on any more crazy car chases."

"It's okay. I kind of enjoyed it. I've never been in a car chase before," he said. Suddenly he laughed. "I should have known something was wrong when you said the kidnapper was driving a Volvo. How many car chase scenes do you see in movies where they say, 'Follow that Volvo'?"

I started to laugh, too. "At least you didn't end up with anything on your shirt today," I joked.

The laughter drained from his face. "Oh, no!" he said. "Charlene was waiting for me by the front entrance. Boy, is she ever going to be mad!"

Chapter 7

As we swung into the parking lot we could see Charlene standing by the front gate with her hands on her hips. She didn't look very happy. In fact, if looks could kill, I wouldn't be around to tell you this story.

"Okay, what was it this time?" she demanded as soon as Drew climbed out of the car. "She squeezed a ketchup bottle all over you? She hit you on the head with the *Encyclopaedia Britannica* and you had to go to the emergency room?" Drew just grinned at her, which seemed to make Charlene even more furious. "It better be something pretty important to leave me standing here with no ride home."

"I'm sorry, Charlene, I totally forgot about you," Drew said.

That wasn't the smartest thing to say under the circumstances.

Charlene turned an interesting shade of purple. "Oh, that's just great," she sputtered. "Did Little Miss Accident-prone here drive me out of your mind?"

"I didn't mean it like that," he said. "It was an emergency. Roni witnessed a kidnapping and we had to go check it out."

"If there was any justice in the world, someone would have kidnapped her," Charlene said.

"Charlene," Drew snapped. "You don't seem to get it. A kid's life might have been in danger. It was very brave of her to try to help."

I looked at him with a grateful smile. He wasn't going to tell her how stupid I'd been.

"So what happened?" Even Charlene was a little interested by now.

"The boy was handed back to his mother," Drew said with satisfaction.

"No kidding? Is this going to be in the papers or something?"

"Oh, no," Drew said. "We didn't want to give our names. We let the police take over."

"You could have gotten shot," Charlene said.

"You have to take some risks in life," Drew said. He caught my expression and winked. I had to press my lips together to keep from giggling.

"Well, are you all done now?" Charlene asked. "Do

you have any more superhero jobs to do before you can take me home? Any runaway circus elephants to stop before we can all sleep safely in our beds?"

"No, I think I've done enough for one day," he said.

"Good, because I was about to call my father for a ride, and I know he would have been awfully mad if he had to drive all the way into the city for me."

That reminded me that I had no ride, either. I looked at my watch. "Oh, no," I said. "I missed my bus. How am I going to get home?"

"Call your parents, the way I was going to," Charlene said.

"Where do you live?" Drew cut in.

"Out toward Oak Creek."

"I'll give you a ride. We're heading that way," he said.

"Drew!" Charlene hissed. "Could I have a word with you, please?"

She dragged him aside. She had lowered her voice, but I could hear enough of the words to get her drift. "I do not want to ride home with her in the car . . . are you out of your mind . . . geeky freshman . . ."

I stood there, half in and half out of the car, feeling trapped and awkward. I wanted to get out and say, "It's all right. I can get my own ride home." But I knew that I couldn't. My dad didn't get back from work until almost seven.

Drew opened his car door. "Get in the back seat if you want a ride home, Charlene," he said pointedly.

"You want me to sit in the back seat?" Charlene gasped. She looked ready to explode.

"Just this once. Roni's already got all her stuff in the front."

"It's okay. I can move," I said.

"Stay where you are." Drew put out his hand to stop me.

Charlene climbed into the back seat, glaring at me. "Roni, is that her name?" she asked him. "Why does that sound so familiar? Oh, now I remember." She looked at me and gave a high-pitched laugh. "You were the one who went to guys' PE on the first day of school. You really are totally clueless, aren't you?"

"Charlene, that's not nice," Drew said.

"You laughed about it more than anyone," Charlene reminded him. "You were the one who called her a dweeb."

"Charlene!" Drew said again. "Just shut up, okay?"

"Fine," Charlene said. "Be nice to her if you want, but don't be surprised if you find your grades wiped off the computer or you slip on something she spills and break your leg. I could tell she was bad news the minute I saw her."

I sat in the front seat wishing I were anyplace else on earth. Part of me was glad that Drew was actually taking my side, even though I knew he probably *had* laughed about me behind my back and he probably would again tomorrow. But one thing I decided was that I'd had enough of letting Charlene walk all over me. Something told me that if I didn't stand up for myself now, they'd think I was a dweeb forever.

"Actually, I went to guys' PE on purpose," I said calmly. "I wanted to check out the freshman guys, and that seemed like the quickest way of doing it."

"Really?" Drew asked.

"Yeah, and I would have pulled it off, only I didn't want to start wrestling with the tubs of lard in that class."

Drew chuckled.

"Is that why you threw your lunch all over Drew— to check out the sophomore guys?" Charlene asked icily. "Because if so, you're wasting your time. All the cute ones are taken."

"I'm not the one sitting in the back seat," I said. I heard Charlene gasp. I thought I saw Drew grin again, but I decided to shut up. I'd already done enough damage for one day.

City blocks sped past. I'd never ridden in a convertible before today. I was surprised how little wind you got in the front seat. Glancing at Charlene, I saw that this wasn't true of the back seat. Her hair was blowing all over the place. She kept trying to hold it down, but she wasn't succeeding.

"So, Roni, where do you live?" Drew asked.

Suddenly it hit me. He was going to drive me to my house. He was going to see the neighborhood I lived in. He was going to hear the loud Latin music blaring from radios up and down the street. He was going to see little kids playing in the dirt and smell chili cooking in every house. I already knew Charlene's opinion of Mexicans, and I knew I didn't want Drew and Charlene to see my neighborhood. It would just be one more thing for her to despise me for.

"Oh, not too far from here," I said. "If you drop me off at the Twin Oaks Center, I can walk from there."

"That's okay, I'll run you home. It's no problem," Drew said.

I had to think fast. What would be the nearest acceptable neighborhood? "Actually I live in Regency Estates," I blurted.

"You do?"

"That's right." The impressive brick gateway to the estates was coming up on our right. "You can turn in here."

"Okay." He swung the car in between the banks of flowers surrounding the entrance. Mini-palaces loomed ahead of us. I had to decide which one I would claim as my home. Nothing too fancy. I tried to look for a more modest house—one with only one turret and no pillars.

"There, that's it," I said. "The one on the corner there."

"The one on the corner?" Drew sounded surprised, but he pulled up anyway.

Charlene let out a delighted laugh. "See, what did I tell you? She's a total phony."

"Charlene, be quiet . . ." Drew began.

I got out. "Thanks very much for the ride," I said.

"Why should I be quiet?" Charlene continued. "Why shouldn't she know that she really blew it this time?" She turned to me with a triumphant smile. "This isn't your house, is it?"

"How do you know?" I stammered.

"Because it's Drew's house, that's how," she said, laughing loudly. "This is so funny. I can't wait to tell the gang about it."

I prayed for the ground to open up and swallow me. When it didn't, I started running, as fast as I could, out of Regency Estates, with the sound of Charlene's mocking laughter still ringing in my ears.

This time I couldn't tell Abuela what had happened, because that would mean explaining why I had needed another address in the first place. I knew my family wouldn't understand why I was suddenly ashamed of my neighborhood. In fact, they'd be horrified. I didn't think I could handle a lecture on being proud of my culture on top of everything else. They'd never understand that I *was* proud of my heritage, in theory. It was just right now, at this time in my life, I thought it would be better if nobody knew I was a Latina. So I sprinted for the phone and called Ginger.

"I'm not going to school, ever again," I told her.

"What happened this time?" she said with a laugh. "It can't be worse than the other things."

"Oh, no?" I said. Then I told her.

When I'd finished, she was silent for a minute. "You're right," she said finally. "That is probably a combination of the most embarrassing things that can happen to a person in one afternoon—apart from your clothes falling off in the middle of Macy's."

"Don't say it!" I wailed. "That will probably happen tomorrow. Do you think I can get my parents to let me transfer back to school here?"

"You want to go to Las Lomas High, where you'd have to take home ec while the boys have wood shop?" Ginger asked incredulously. "Roni, Alta Mesa is a good school. You can't seriously be thinking of quitting because of a few embarrassing incidents."

"I am serious. I don't know how I'm going to face anyone tomorrow," I said. "You can be sure Charlene will tell all her friends and it will be all around school."

"So they might laugh for a few minutes," Ginger said. "But you've got us. We'll stand up for you, Roni. And you have to stand up for yourself, too. You never let anyone walk all over you back in middle school."

"I know," I said, "but it's different here."

88

"What I can't understand," Ginger said slowly, "is why you did such a dumb thing in the first place. I mean, why would you tell anyone you lived in Regency Estates?"

I felt myself going hot all over. My family was in the next room, probably listening to every word. "I didn't want them to see where I live," I whispered into the phone.

"Roni Ruiz, I'm surprised at you!" Ginger exclaimed. "You can't be ashamed of who you are!"

"I'm not," I said. "At least, I didn't think I was until I heard Charlene talking about creepy Mexicans. I just thought she'd have something else to look down on me for if she saw my neighborhood."

"That's not like you at all," Ginger said. "Who was the loudest person at Cinco de Mayo celebrations at our old school?"

"People at our old school knew what Cinco de Mayo was." I gave a big sigh. "I don't know what's happened to me since we started Alta Mesa. I don't know who I am anymore, or who I want to be. I'm so confused, Ginger."

"Be the person you've always been," Ginger said firmly. "Be Veronica Consuela Ruiz—a fun, smart, sassy girl and my best friend."

I felt tears well into my eyes. "Thanks, Ginger," I said. "I guess I needed a confidence boost right now."

"So I'll meet you at the usual time in the morning."

"Okay. Only, I think I'll lie low for a while. You guys have to help me hide out where Charlene and Drew can't find me."

"You're so weird sometimes," Ginger said, laughing as she hung up the phone.

Chapter

8

I managed to stay invisible all morning. I made my friends walk like a solid wall in front of me so that I'd have time to turn and run if I saw Charlene or Drew coming toward me. But our paths didn't cross until lunchtime.

There was a big rally in the quad because we had a football game that night against our archrivals. All the cheerleaders and football players were in uniform. The pep band was there, and lots of people were dressed in our school colors of blue and white. For the first time I felt excited, as if I actually belonged at this place. I'd heard about pep rallies, but I'd never been to one before.

We were walking through the halls at the beginning of lunch hour and people behind us were chanting, "When I say Alta, you say Mesa . . . Alta Mesa, Alta Mesa. When I say blue, you say white . . . When I say number, you say one . . ." Karen linked arms with me and Ginger and we marched in step, laughing, as Justine rolled her eyes and followed us. That's when I saw Drew, coming out of a side hall with his football buddies, heading for the quad.

I yelped in fear, wrenched myself loose from Karen and Ginger, and fled into the nearest classroom. "See you later, guys. Gotta go," I called. I saw their bewildered faces as I closed the door behind me.

It didn't occur to me that the room might be occupied—most classrooms are empty at lunchtime. So my heart nearly leaped out of my chest when I heard a voice behind me say delightedly, "Roni! What a pleasant surprise. Have you come to join us?"

I turned around slowly. A whole roomful of nerds was looking at me. It was terrifying. Was it possible that there was a nerd club on campus?

I started to back toward the door. "Is . . . uh . . . something going on in here?" I asked. My voice came out high and tight.

"Yes, it's the weekly meeting of the computer club. I hope you've come to join us," Ronald said, beaming at Owen. "We don't get too many girls interested in building an IBM clone, which is our special project for this semester." Somehow, I didn't think it was the special project that kept girls away from this club.

Ronald was heading toward me, smiling his repulsive smile. "Can I show you how far we've gotten?" he asked. I was paralyzed. Outside in the hall I still might run into Drew and his buddies. Inside this room I would be studying an IBM clone with about twenty nerds. Which was worse?

I started babbling. "Gee, I'm sorry, Ronald. I must have the wrong room. I was looking for the ballet club. You don't know where they're meeting, do you? I'm hopeless with computers, I'm afraid. I don't know bits from bytes . . . ha, ha. Well, gotta go. Got to practice my *pas de deux* . . ."

Just before he had a chance to grab my arm and drag me to a fate worse than death, I opened the door and ran out. I ran all the way to the quad, which was now filled with students. Drew and the other football players were sitting on the platform at one end. I looked for Ginger, Karen, and Justine among the mass of students, but the crowd was too tightly packed for me to see where they were. So I just sort of hid myself behind a bush.

At least, I thought I was hidden.

"And now for the famous ice-cream-eating contest," Jeff Parker, student body president, was announcing. "For this annual event we need six football players, who will go select six lovely female volunteers from the audience."

A wave of excited giggles ran through the crowd.

"Not me, I'm wearing good clothes," I heard a girl beside me say.

"I came prepared. I've got on an old T-shirt," her friend answered.

I didn't hear anything after that, because the football players were coming down from the stage and Drew was heading in my direction. There had to be some mistake. Drew would never choose me as a partner, not with Charlene watching, not after all the things I had done. But he kept on coming until he was right in front of me. He took my hand.

"Congratulations, Roni. You get to be my partner," he said.

I was in a daze as I was led onto the stage. I could feel Drew's hand, warm and firm holding mine. It was a miracle.

Drew led me across the stage, still holding my hand in front of zillions of people, and sat me in a chair. Then he sat in a chair facing mine. I saw five other girls with the same dazed looks on their faces sitting opposite five other football heroes. I couldn't understand why Drew had picked me. Maybe my crazy stunts had touched his heart after all. Maybe he liked way-out girls.

"Okay, lucky contestants," Jeff was saying. "The winner of this contest is the first football player who can feed his partner a bowl of ice cream." Cheerleaders came around with big bowls of strawberry ice cream and large plastic spoons.

"Easy, you say? But wait, there's more."

A great roar of laughter went up as the cheerleaders started to blindfold the football players. Then they put big plastic bibs on the victims.

"Check the blindfolds so that they can't cheat," Jeff instructed. "All ready? Okay, on your marks, get set, go!"

Drew stuck the spoon in the ice cream and then in my general direction. I tried to connect it with my mouth, but it was a large spoon, and most of it went on my face. The rest went down my front in a cold blob. Drew was already digging for the next load. He swung and this time it splattered in my hair. I could hear the crowd screaming encouragement.

By the fourth or fifth spoonful I was pretty much covered in ice cream. It was obvious by now that Drew wasn't even trying to find my mouth. He was just hurling ice cream at me and enjoying it. There wasn't much I could do but be a good sport. I put on a big, fake smile while I sat there, opened my mouth, and waited for the next faceful.

I kept on smiling until, after what seemed like an eternity, someone down the line won. Everyone cheered. Blindfolds were taken off. They took off my bib, but it hadn't done much good. My face and my shorts and my hair were now plastered with sticky strawberry goop.

"Let's have a big hand for our brave contestants,"

Jeff said. There was more cheering. I got up. Drew was looking at me, half-amused, half-embarrassed.

"I wasn't too accurate with my spoon, was I?" he asked.

I looked at him calmly. "It's okay. I understand why you picked me," I said. "I guess that makes us even now."

Then I walked off the stage with as much dignity as I could muster and went to clean up. People came up to me and said I was a good sport and joked about how I'd never want to eat strawberry ice cream again. Ginger, Karen, and Justine found me in the bathroom and tried to help get the worst of it out of my hair. But I felt sticky and uncomfortable all afternoon. I also felt like I might cry if anything else went wrong.

When the final bell rang, I just wanted to slip out of school before one more person asked me what had happened to my hair and why my white shirt had one pink sleeve. I was walking out of the administration building with my friends when the nerds appeared in that stealthy way of theirs.

"Quick, hurry," I muttered, grabbing Ginger's arm. "If there's one thing I can't face now, it's—"

"Hi, Roni!" Owen called. Ronald, Walter, and Wolfgang came running after him, scattering pens from their briefcases as they ran. "We just want to tell you," Owen said, "that we really admired you up on the stage today. We caught your act just as we were coming out of our computer club meeting."

"Yeah, Roni," Wolfgang agreed. "It takes a big person to keep on smiling while someone throws ice cream at her."

"Thanks," I muttered.

"Those football players think they're gods, just because they made the team," Owen said. "They don't care how they make people like us feel, as long as they get a laugh."

I wasn't sure that I wanted to put myself together in a category with Owen or Ronald, but I was touched that they were so mad on my behalf. After all, they couldn't help looking, talking, and acting weird, could they? They were also warm and sensitive and their hearts were in the right place.

"Thanks, guys," I said.

"Will you be okay?" Owen asked. "We could help clean you up."

I had a terrifying mental image of me in a bathroom being scrubbed by four nerds. "Uh . . . no, thanks. I have to get my bus right now. But thanks for the offer," I said.

Ginger and I were just about to leave when we heard a burst of loud laughter. The frosh-soph football team ran out of the locker room toward their waiting bus. I saw Drew look in my direction and I immediately dodged behind the closest bush. To my

97

horror, he didn't head for the bus at all but came over to my friends.

"I thought I saw Roni," I heard him say.

"Who?" Ginger began innocently, but Wolfgang was too fast for her.

"Roni?" he said loudly. "She just went behind that bush."

"Wolfgang!" Justine hissed, but the damage was already done. The nerds might have been warm and sensitive, but they were also totally clueless! I heard footsteps. Drew pulled aside a branch and peered in at me.

"Hi," he said.

"Hi."

We looked at each other. I could see him taking in my matted hair and my pink-stained clothing.

"I couldn't leave without saying I was sorry," he said. "It started out as a joke. Charlene suggested it, but I've been feeling bad all afternoon. You didn't even yell at me, and I wrecked your shirt."

"It's okay. I didn't like it anyway," I said, managing a weak smile.

"I have to go to the game," he said. "Are you coming to watch?" he asked, glancing across at the bus.

I shook my head. "I'd like to, but I don't have a ride home afterward," I said. Then, in case he thought this was a hint, I added, "My parents are expecting me home."

He nodded. "Well, maybe I'll see you around this weekend. After all, we live so close to each other, in Regency Estates," he said with a knowing smile.

"I . . . uh, don't live in Regency Estates," I admitted. "I just wanted you to think I did. Dumb, huh?"

"It's okay," he said. "Forget it. You do live somewhere around me, don't you?"

I nodded.

"So maybe we will see each other, then."

Could this be an invitation? Was Drew actually suggesting that he'd like to see me this weekend?

"Drew, get over here!" someone yelled from the bus.

He grinned. "Gotta go. Wish me luck."

"Take care," I called as he ran across the yard with big, easy strides.

"He came over to apologize," I said to my friends, who were staring after Drew with disapproving looks on their faces.

"It's about time," Karen said. "That creep ruined a good shirt."

"Not that good," Justine said. "It wasn't silk or anything."

"Justine!" we all yelled in unison.

"Sorry," Justine muttered.

"He also came over to say we should do something this weekend," I added, savoring the looks on my friends' faces.

"Are you kidding?" Karen asked.

"I don't think so," I replied. "He actually said that maybe we'd see each other, since we lived so close."

"That sounds promising," Ginger said. "Maybe it was worth getting ice cream in your hair after all."

"But the guy's a jerk, Ginger," Karen argued. "What he did to Roni was so mean. I think she should forget about him."

"I agree," Justine said. "I mean, just because the guy's drop-dead cute with the longest eyelashes in Arizona doesn't mean that a girl can forget that he acted like a jerk."

"Yes, she can," Ginger and I said at exactly the same time.

We looked at each other and grinned.

"Seriously, Justine, he did come over to apologize," I said. "In front of the whole team, too. And he was nice about being dragged on my fake kidnapping, and he stuck up for me in front of Charlene. That has to mean something, doesn't it? He's not really a creep."

"Let's face it, she's crazy about him," Ginger said to Justine. "You'd feel the same way if a guy like Drew asked to see you this weekend."

"I guess," Justine said with a shrug. "Speaking of weekends, what fun, fantastic plans do we have?"

"None, so far," Ginger said.

"I have a great idea, then," Justine said.

"What?"

"Let's go to the mall."

"That's a great idea?" I said. "I don't think it wins the prize for most original."

"But we've never been, the four of us together. We could go to one of the big malls in Scottsdale—you know, the kind of place where they let you test the perfume. It's been ages since I bought any new clothes—at least a couple of weeks. I'm suffering from mall-withdrawal symptoms."

"It could be fun," Ginger said.

"And malls are great places to meet guys," Justine added.

"Are you coming, Roni?" Ginger asked.

"I don't know," I said. "What if Drew calls while I'm out?"

"Did you give him your phone number?"

"No."

"Then how can he call you? Does he even know your last name?" Ginger asked.

"I'm not sure," I confessed.

"So come to the mall with us."

"All right," I said. "He didn't actually say he'd call me, anyway. It was more like, 'Maybe we'll run into each other somewhere.' I'd be dumb to sit home waiting while you guys are out having fun. Charlene probably won't let him anywhere near me anyhow."

"How about you, Karen?" Justine asked.

Karen made a face. "I'd love to come. I've hardly ever been to the mall with my friends. Oh, don't look like that, Justine. I know I'm a deprived child. But I don't know if I can make it this weekend. I've got this violin recital coming up . . ."

"Violin recital? Karen, how exciting!" I said.

But Karen didn't look exactly thrilled. "It's no big thing," she said. "But I know my parents will insist I stay home and practice until my fingers fall off."

"Are you going to be one of those people who play Carnegie Hall someday?" Justine asked.

"That's what my parents hope," Karen said. "It's always been their dream for me."

"When is the recital?" Ginger asked. "We all have to come and cheer."

"A week from this Saturday," Karen said. "Let's not talk about it. I'm getting nervous already."

"So you need a break at the mall. It's a great way to fight stress," Justine said. "I know when I'm tense and my stepmother is bugging me, I always head straight for the mall. I feel secure there."

Ginger looked at me and grinned. "Other people go to health clubs, or the mountains, or to church, but Justine goes to the mall."

"I understand," I said. "I feel the same way sometimes. It's like you've escaped to a different world, where you're invisible and protected."

"Right," Justine said.

"Although with my current luck, we'll just be testing our first perfume when we'll find ourselves surrounded by nerds, saying, 'Gee, Roni, you smell nice,' in their squeaky voices."

"No way!" Justine said. "They don't really hang out in the mall, do they?"

"I don't think so," I said. "But maybe one of their computers will tell them that's where we are, and they'll track us there."

"But they won't know which mall," Justine said. "I think we'll be safe enough."

"There's our bus, Roni. Gotta run," Ginger said, dragging me away by the arm.

"We'll call you guys tonight about where to meet!" I shouted over my shoulder. I followed Ginger to the bus and sank into the seat with a happy sigh. This would be a great weekend.

Chapter 9

That night I lay in bed, listening to my two sisters breathing, and thought about Drew. It seemed like my spirits were finally doing their job after all. My first encounters with my dream guy had been weird, to say the least, but now it seemed as if he really might like me. *At least I made him notice me right away,* I thought, smiling now at all my horrible accidents. Maybe attacking him with books and chili was the only way an ordinary person like me could get the attention of a popular guy like him. Abuela was right: things could change from bad to good in a hurry when you were my age.

I went over Drew's words again and again in my mind. Was he just being friendly when he said he might see me this weekend, or was that his way of saying that he wanted to? Was I supposed to pick up his cue and tell him where I'd be so that he could just happen to bump into me? I wished I knew more about the rules of the dating game.

I closed my eyes and let myself slip into a wonderful fantasy in which Drew drove by in his red convertible and swept me up into it. We sped along winding mountain roads with my hair blowing in the wind. At last we came to a mountaintop and parked overlooking the city, and Drew slipped his arm around my shoulders. I rested my head against him and then he turned to kiss me . . . I sighed so loudly that Monica woke up and turned over with a groan. *Back to reality,* I thought.

My friends and I had arranged to meet in Scottsdale at two-thirty on Saturday. I got up late and washed my hair. I almost wished now that I hadn't cut it this summer. I'd done it to get back at my mother for making me wear old-fashioned skirts to school. Most of the time I liked my new short, bouncy look. But I'd also heard that guys liked girls with long hair. Oh, well, there wasn't much I could do about that now. It would probably take me years to grow it again. At least it would be clean and shiny if I ran into Drew today.

When I came down to the kitchen after my shower, I found my mother furiously making tortillas again.

"Mom, why don't you just tell Abuela that we always buy our tortillas?" I whispered. "You don't have time to do this every day."

"She wouldn't understand, Roni," my mother said. "She'd just think I was lazy."

"Here, I'll help you," I said. "Show me what to do."

"You can help me by making sure your sisters have something nice to wear," she said. "I'm taking them to a birthday party this afternoon. That reminds me, I hope you don't mind staying with Paco and your grandmother for a little while."

"This afternoon? But Mama, I have plans for this afternoon."

"What plans? You didn't mention anything to me."

"We only decided last night. I'm meeting my friends at the mall."

"Oh, well . . ." she began. Clearly this didn't count as an important plan in her mind. "You can go to the mall anytime."

"But this is different, Mama. I've never been to the mall with my new friends."

She shrugged. Nobody in the world could do a better, bigger shrug than my mama. "I'm sorry, Roni, but what can I do? I've already accepted the invitation to the birthday party for the girls, and I can't take Paco to that."

"Can't Papa drive them?"

"Papa is refereeing a soccer game all afternoon."

"Then can't you leave Paco with Abuela?"

"Roni, be sensible. She can barely walk, and that child moves like lightning. I don't like leaving her alone for more than a few minutes, either. She's not too steady on her feet. You'll just have to call your friends and tell them you can't make it after all."

"This isn't fair," I said angrily. "I'm always the one who's stuck. I'll never fit in at my new school if you don't let me do the things everyone else does."

"I said I was sorry, Veronica," my mother said calmly, "but you didn't let me know in advance, and family does have to come first."

"I don't see why," I muttered under my breath. I stomped across the room to the phone. I was really angry. In my mind, I was going through all the ways I'd get back at Mama. I'd tell Abuela that she didn't make her own tortillas!

My friends were very sympathetic. "Oh, that's too bad, Roni. Poor you, stuck baby-sitting all afternoon," Karen said. "And after I managed to convince my parents that I needed new school supplies from the mall, too."

"Why don't you put the kid to bed and sneak out?" Justine suggested. Obviously she hadn't done much baby-sitting in her life. Kids don't just go to bed when you want them to.

"You could always take Paco out to play in the

front yard in case Drew happened to be driving by, looking for you," Ginger said helpfully.

I knew she was trying to cheer me up, but I was pretty sure that Drew wouldn't be driving down my street. Why would he come to a Mexican neighborhood?

After lunch I helped dress my little sisters in their frilly party dresses and put bows in their hair. They looked really adorable as they sat in the back seat of the car, trying not to move in case they creased their skirts. Then I went back inside to Abuela and Paco. My grandmother was dozing in her chair, the way she usually did in the afternoon.

"Why don't you take a nap, too?" I suggested to Paco.

"Not tired," he said, and started pushing his toy cars all over the floor, making loud car and truck sounds.

I sat on the sofa, feeling like a martyr.

Around two-thirty there was a knock at the front door. My heart leaped. Had Drew found out where I lived and come to visit me? I was dying to see Drew, but I didn't want him to see me here, among my eccentric relatives in my weird house.

In a panic I started throwing things into the toy box and plumping pillows on the couch. Then I sprinted into my bedroom and brushed my hair. Then I remembered I hadn't put on any makeup, so I ran back to put on lipstick. Then I took a deep breath, put on what I hoped was a gorgeous smile, and opened the front door.

"Surprise!" yelled three voices outside. There stood Karen, Ginger, and Justine, beaming at me.

"Wh-what are you doing here?" I stammered.

"We felt sorry for you stuck at home, so we decided to come keep you company," Karen said.

"Yeah, we can go to the mall anytime," Justine added. "Aren't you going to invite us in?"

I realized that I was standing with my hand firmly on the doorknob, blocking the doorway. I was overwhelmed by what nice friends I had, but it was beginning to sink in that Karen and Justine would now have to see my house and family, whether I wanted them to or not. "Sure," I said hesitantly. "Come on in."

"You don't sound overjoyed to see us," Ginger commented. "Justine gave up her first shopping trip in two weeks for you."

"I know," I said, "and I am glad to see you. It's just that . . . my grandmother's sleeping right now. Let's go sit on the patio."

I took them around the side of the house to the shady patio at the back. Our big black dog, Midnight, got up and wagged his tail.

"Oh, this is so neat!" Karen exclaimed, looking at the grapevine my father had trained over the patio, where it now provided leafy shade. "Look, there are even grapes growing on it," she added.

"I'll make us all some lemonade," I said.

At that moment Paco appeared and was instantly snapped up by Karen and Justine.

"Oh, isn't he adorable!" cried Karen.

"Hi, cutie pie. What's your name?" Justine cooed.

Ginger, who had known him since he was born and had had plenty of chances to see that Paco wasn't always adorable, sank into the most comfortable chair.

"He doesn't speak much English yet," I apologized. *"Di les como tu llames,"* I said to him.

"Paco," he said.

"Hi, Paco, I'm Justine," she said. "Is that your truck?"

Suddenly it didn't seem to matter that Paco's English mostly came from TV shows, or that my friends only knew a few words of Spanish. They were communicating. I went to get the lemonade. When I came back, Ginger, Karen, and Justine were whispering together. They looked up as I walked onto the porch.

"Ginger just had a brilliant idea," Karen said. "How about if we baby-sit while you go visit Drew?"

"Me? Visit Drew?"

"Yeah. You want to, don't you?" Ginger said. "He did say you might see each other this weekend."

"Yeah, but . . ." I hesitated. "It's quite a walk."

"So ride over there on your bike."

110

"Yeah, Roni. You'll just be cruising around the neighborhood, and if he happens to come out, or drive past, then you act really surprised," Justine said.

"Then you'd find out if he really did want to get together with you this weekend," Ginger added.

"Wow," I said, still trying to digest this. "I don't know, guys. I mean, my little brother and my grandmother . . . they don't speak much English, you know."

"Hi, my name is Paco," Paco said in perfect English. "I'm adorable."

My friends all burst out laughing. "I think we'll do just fine," Ginger said. "And you'll only be away a little while."

"I'm not sure about this," I said.

"You do want to see if Drew really likes you, right?" Justine asked.

"Yeah . . ." I was going hot all over at the thought of riding past Drew's house. What would he think if he came out and saw me? But hadn't he suggested we might run into each other? At least I'd be able to tell if he was happy to see me. "Well, okay, I guess," I said. "Let me go change and tell my grandmother, if she's awake."

"What do we do if she wakes up and calls for you?" Karen asked.

"Find out what she wants," Justine said quickly. "I speak Spanish, remember."

"Justine," Ginger said, laughing. "We're in your Spanish class. You got the words for horse and hair mixed up!"

"Only because I speak pure Castilian Spanish that I learned in Spain. It's different there," Justine said grandly.

"You don't have to worry," I told them. "She usually dozes for a few hours in the afternoon, so I think we're safe. I'll tell Paco where I'm going."

I told him quickly in Spanish that the girls were going to baby-sit him.

"I know that," he said scornfully, making me realize that he understood a lot more English than I thought. I ran into the house. Abuela was still sleeping. I took off my old clothes and put on my white shorts and my new halter top. When I came out of my room, Abuela's eyes were open.

"Abuelita, I'm going out for just a few minutes," I said. "My friends are here and they're going to watch Paco."

"You're going out dressed like that?" Abuela asked. "Where are you going, dressed in beach clothes?"

"Oh, I'm just riding my bike over to say hello to a friend."

"On the streets? You're riding your bicycle on the streets in a bathing suit?"

"It's a halter top, Abuela. They're in style."

"They don't hide much of the body," she said. "It's

head. I looked up, straight into Charlene's cold blue eyes.

"What are you doing?" she demanded.

I decided that I wasn't going to let her push me around. Whatever I was doing outside Drew's house was none of her business. "It's a free country, isn't it?" I said. "I can ride my bike on a public street."

A mocking smile spread across her face. "You're wasting your time, you know," she said.

"I don't know what you're talking about."

"Sure you do," she said in a voice dripping with sarcasm. "You're hanging around Drew's house because you want him to come out and notice you. But I can tell you right now that he wouldn't notice you if you were the last girl in Arizona. He thinks you're a big joke and a big pain, that's all."

I fought to keep my cool. "Oh," I said, "is that why he suggested we get together this weekend?"

"In your dreams," she said, still smirking.

"It's a pity you weren't there, or you would have heard him saying how convenient it was that we lived close to each other," I said.

Charlene came toward me, her eyes sparking dangerously now. "Let me make one thing very clear to you, Roni, or whatever your name is: Drew already has a girlfriend. He's a naturally friendly guy. He talks to everyone, but that doesn't mean that he's interested in you. Drew and I are a couple,

115

and it's going to stay that way. So butt out of our lives, or I can make things real unpleasant for you at school."

"Is that how you hang on to Drew, by threatening him?" I said.

"Get out of here right now," Charlene snapped. "Drew's busy working on a paper for school. His mom just sent me home so he could finish it, so there's no way he'd want to be interrupted by anyone else. Now beat it!"

She stood there, arms folded, on the path between me and the front door. I didn't know what to do. She looked so furious that I was afraid to try pushing past her. I had no intention of causing any more big scenes in front of Drew, and I didn't want him mad at me for keeping him from doing his homework. *Okay,* I thought, *I can wait. If he really wants to see me, he'll find another chance.*

"I'm leaving," I said. "Tell Drew I said hi and I'll see him later." I gave her a sweet smile.

My mission hadn't exactly been a success, but it hadn't been a total failure, either. I could tell that I had Charlene worried. I didn't usually have a very high opinion of girls who stole other girls' guys, but in this case . . . well, all was fair in love and war! And Charlene had made it very clear that it was war between us. Surely Drew had to be getting tired of a demanding, possessive girl like Charlene, even if she was gorgeous and popular. What he needed was a sweet, understanding, undemanding girl who would make him laugh—a girl like me.

It was only as I got on my bike to ride home that I remembered I had let the air out of the front tire.

Chapter

10

I was hot and sweaty by the time I arrived at my house, wheeling my bike along the dusty road. My thoughts were fixed on our cool patio and that big jug of lemonade. I knew the others would be dying to hear what had happened at Drew's house.

"Okay, guys, *The Roni and Drew Saga,* chapter one, full report," I said, pushing open the back gate. The patio was empty.

The scene was was like something out of the twilight zone: Paco's cars were scattered around; the lemonade and glasses were on the table. The glasses were half-empty, and there was even a dent in the pillows where somebody had recently sat. But no one was there.

"Hello!" I yelled. "Ginger? Karen? Justine? Paco? Where is everyone?"

Oh, no, I thought with rising panic. *Abuela got sick and they rushed her to the hospital, and I'm going to be in big trouble for taking off and leaving her.*

At that moment Karen's worried face peeked around the back door. "Psst, Roni, over here," she whispered.

My friends were clustered in a tight little knot, just inside the kitchen.

"What's wrong?" I asked.

"Your grandmother's still sleeping and we've been trying not to wake her," Justine said. "We didn't want her to worry."

"About what?"

"Promise not to panic," Karen said, holding up her hand.

"Not to panic about what?"

"We lost Paco."

"You what?" My voice echoed across the patio.

"Shhh," the others said in unison.

"My little brother is lost? I was only gone half an hour. How could you do this to me?"

"We can't understand it either," Karen said. "We didn't take our eyes off him for a second. The back gate was shut all the time, and he was playing with his little cars. Then suddenly Justine said, 'Where's Paco?' And he wasn't there. We've searched every-where, Roni. We've been all over the house. What are we going to do?"

119

"Wait a minute," I said. "Did you check the dog-house?"

"The doghouse?" Justine said. "Roni, there's a large dog in there."

I was already sprinting to the big wood-shingled doghouse along the side fence. Midnight got up, wagging his tail as I approached. There behind him, curled up on the dog's mat, sound asleep, was Paco.

"Come out of there," I said, dragging him, still half-asleep, into the sunlight. "You were very bad to hide in there and scare my friends."

I looked up apologetically at them. "I'm sorry," I said. "He goes in there sometimes, usually when he's hiding from my mother. He probably wanted to play a trick on you, but then he got comfortable and fell asleep."

My friends were already laughing.

"You should have seen us, Roni," Ginger said, "crawling around your grandmother on our hands and knees and whispering for Paco so that we didn't wake her up!"

"We thought she'd panic if she found out he was missing," Justine added. "We looked everywhere—all the kitchen closets, the linen hampers . . . we were getting really desperate."

"I'm glad you came back so quickly," Karen agreed. "I guess Drew wasn't home, huh?"

"He was home all right," I said, "but I didn't get to see him."

"You chickened out at the last minute?" Justine asked.

"No, I was prevented by a fierce watchdog named Charlene," I said. "I don't think she likes me very much."

"Would you like someone who's making a really obvious play for your boyfriend?" Ginger asked. "I mean, she's not going to say, 'Please help yourself to Drew, Roni.'"

Karen and Justine laughed, but Ginger's words stirred up the guilt I was trying to pretend I didn't feel.

"I know," I said. "I'm having some problems with that, too. But it's not as if we're best friends or anything. And I don't have a real chance with Drew. I mean, she's gorgeous and blond and popular and I'm . . . I'm me. Obviously I'm as different from Charlene as I could possibly be, which means I'm not Drew's type. It's just my wildest dream that Drew will notice me someday. I have to go for it."

"Oh, I think he's noticed you," Justine said.

"In a positive way, I mean," I said. "Do you think it's wrong of me to even think about another girl's boyfriend?"

"No way," Karen said. "Charlene's already told you that you don't have a chance. So prove her wrong."

"And she sounds like a big pain," Ginger agreed,

"especially after what she said about Mexican people. I'd say she doesn't deserve a cute boyfriend."

"You've got to find a way to get rid of her, Roni," Justine said seriously.

"Apart from kidnapping, what do you suggest?"

"Send her a letter that says she's won a cheerleading contest and the first prize is a month in Alaska," Karen suggested.

"Put purple dye in her shampoo!"

We all laughed together as we drank the rest of the lemonade.

"You have to take us on a tour of your house now, Roni," Karen said. "You have so many interesting things."

I looked from Karen's smiling face to Justine's. Even Justine wasn't turning up her nose. They really found my house interesting!

"Yeah, Roni, I wanted to know more about the statue in the corner. Karen has been to Catholic school for hundreds of years and she couldn't even tell us what it was," Justine said.

"I don't know one saint from another," Karen said. "But I want to know where those old onyx carvings come from. They look like Mayan gods or something."

"Okay, follow me," I said, getting up from my seat. "The guided tour of the Ruiz house is about to start."

I didn't see Drew that weekend, even though I cruised around a lot on my bike. But I wasn't too bothered by it—it had been a pretty good weekend in other ways. For one thing, I'd survived my friends' seeing my house. Justine hadn't even commented that it looked like something out of *National Geographic*. In fact, she and Karen had seemed to like it.

"Did Paco recover from sleeping in the doghouse?" Ginger asked as we sat under our tree at lunchtime on Monday.

"He does it all the time," I said. "He likes it in there. He's always pretending to be a puppy. I'm sorry, but I have a weird family."

"I thought he was adorable," Justine said.

"We didn't think he was so adorable when we were crawling all over the house whispering his name," Ginger added. "You'd never believe where we looked."

"I thought of looking in the doghouse, but the dog was there and I didn't know how fierce he might be if we tried to disturb him," Justine said.

"Justine, you did not!" Ginger said. "You were the one who kept on saying, 'I know he's been kidnapped and we're going to get in big trouble.'"

Justine grinned sheepishly. "I wish we'd met your little sisters, too," she said. "You're so lucky to have a big family."

"Lucky? That wouldn't be my word for it," I said.

"What would be your word?"

"Try slave," I said. "I get stuck with all the chores because I'm the oldest. It's always, 'Roni will help you with that,' or 'Don't worry, Roni will clean up the mess.' Cinderella Roni, that's me."

"Oh, yeah, we're so sorry for you," Ginger said sarcastically. She turned to the others. "I've known her all her life, and her mom was always making her new dresses and playing with her hair. I was so jealous."

"Of me?" I asked. I never knew that before.

"Sure. You had a mom to make you look pretty. I just had a house full of guys to tease me and bully me."

"At least you had big brothers to play football with," I said. "I have to play magic princesses with my sisters."

"You two are both lucky because you have brothers and sisters," Justine said. "I hate being an only child. It means that your parents have no one else to blame for anything. And they want to see every piece of homework you do, and they give you the third degree every time you come in the door—"

"And they try to live your life for you," Karen interjected fiercely.

We all looked at her, surprised. Karen usually spoke in a soft, gentle voice. She gave an embarrassed grin when she saw our shocked expressions. "I'm sorry," she said. "I guess I'm really uptight about this recital."

"It's this Saturday, isn't it?" I asked.

Karen wrinkled her nose and nodded. "I wish it was over."

"I'm sure you'll do fine," Ginger said. "I hear you're already the star of the school orchestra."

"I don't mind playing in an orchestra," Karen said, "but I hate being onstage alone. I feel like I'm going to die of stage fright. And this is just a little recital at my music school. My parents keep talking about entering me for competitions and taking me to play in New York and Moscow one day. I just couldn't do it."

"Maybe you'll get more confident as you go along," Ginger said kindly.

Karen shook her head. "I've been taking lessons since I was four," she said. "I hated playing for other people even then. I just don't think I was born to be a performer—at least not a solo performer."

"Then don't do it if you don't like it," Justine said. "Just tell your folks to butt out or you'll quit violin."

Karen looked at her with big, surprised eyes. "Not do it? You don't know my parents very well," she said. "This is their dream for me. If I tell them I'm scared, they just nod and smile and then go on as if I haven't said anything. Or they start babbling about the honor of our family and how proud I've made them. It's very hard." She looked at me. "I'm sure Roni understands. Her parents are old-fashioned like mine. They expect you to obey them, don't they, Roni?"

"You'd better believe it," I said. "But don't worry

125

about Saturday. We'll all come and give you moral support at your recital if you want us to."

"Would you? I'd like that. It would make it easier if I knew you were there rooting for me."

"Of course we'll come, Karen," Justine said. "We'll sit in the front row and make a big banner saying KAREN IS THE GREATEST, and we'll cheer like crazy when you come out onstage."

Karen looked really worried. Justine laughed. "Just kidding," she said. "We'll be very quiet and well behaved, and we'll applaud politely when you're done."

"Thanks, guys," Karen said. "I feel better already knowing that you're going to be there. I'm so tense, I feel like a violin string about to snap."

Ginger opened her lunch bag. "Here, have a brownie," she said. "They're great for relieving tension."

"They're also three zillion calories," I said.

"Karen doesn't need to worry about that," Justine said enviously.

Karen didn't even seem to be listening to any of us. She just took the brownie with a polite nod and started eating it. She really was a bundle of nerves. I decided that my family wasn't so bad after all. At least they let me quit ballet when I wasn't any good at it. They would never have made me do anything I hated.

At that moment a noisy group of kids came along the path. I recognized some of the guys from Drew's football team. They were laughing loudly. One boy called to us, "What do you call a Chinese fat lady?"

"What?" Ginger and I yelled.

"Won Ton," the boy said, and the whole group roared with laughter.

I grinned at Ginger. She grinned back. "Those dumb Chinese jokes are all over school this week," she said. "Some of them are really funny."

"I don't think that's very nice of you guys," Karen said in a stiff voice.

"But Karen," I said, "you're not Chinese. And anyway, they're not mean jokes, they're just silly puns."

"It doesn't matter," Karen said. "Most kids here don't know I'm not Chinese. It's not right to make jokes about any ethnic group."

"I'd agree with you if they were mean jokes," I said, "but those jokes are just fun. They're not really putting anyone down."

"You wouldn't like it if they were Mexican jokes," she said.

"I'm sure I wouldn't mind," I answered, trying to sound more convinced than I really felt. Deep down, a little voice was whispering that I would mind a lot. We'd had some Mexican jokes at my old school. But those were mean jokes, not funny and harmless. "I wouldn't care about innocent jokes like these," I told Karen. "And even if I did, I'd laugh anyway just to show the jokes didn't mean anything."

"I don't like it," Karen said. "There aren't enough

minority kids at this school to make our voices heard. Something like this could start out harmlessly enough, then turn into a big problem. We have to put a stop to it now."

"Come on, Karen, lighten up," I said. "You're totally overreacting. These guys are just having fun. You'll never fit in here if you get upset about little things. The only way we're going to get along at this school is to forget all about ethnic differences and act like regular kids. Nobody's going to like us if we start whining about every little joke."

I looked at Karen. She looked back at me with her dark, solemn eyes for a moment, then turned away. "If that's how you feel," she said quietly.

"Karen, you're just uptight this week because of the recital," I said. "Next week you'll be laughing with the rest of us." I turned to Ginger and Justine. "Did you notice that those guys spoke to us? They're on the football team with Drew. Maybe they saw me talking to him on Friday, and they decided I'm okay."

"That one with the blond curly hair was certainly cute," Justine said. "We'd better do something about getting you and Drew together so that we can meet his friends. It's time for the Boyfriend Club to spring into action. Any suggestions?"

"I think we should go to the game with Roni on Friday night," Ginger said. "That would show her interest in Drew's life and her devotion to him."

"I hardly think he's going to notice me among all those people," I said.

"He'll notice," Ginger said. "He did ask you if you were going to last week's game, didn't he, Roni?"

"Yeah, but I said I had no way of getting home," I said. "The same applies this week, too, unless we can get someone to drive us. We can't all afford taxis like Justine."

"I'll ask if Ben and my brother can give us a ride home," Ginger said. "Their varsity game is right after the frosh-soph game."

"Cool," I said. "That way you get to ride home with Ben, too."

"Do you think I'm stupid?" Ginger said, grinning. "I'd already thought of that."

"Wouldn't it be great if we could double-date one day—you and Ben and me and Drew?" I said dreamily.

"There's one small problem," Justine said, "and her name is Charlene."

"Do you have to remind me?" I asked. "I was trying to forget about her."

"She's not exactly easy to ignore," Justine said, "seeing that she'll be at the game in her cute little uniform, screaming for Drew."

"Maybe a miracle will happen," I said. "Maybe he'll score the winning touchdown and our eyes will meet over the goalpost, and he'll run over to ask me out."

"And then you'll wake up," Justine said.

Chapter 11

"I can't believe it," I whispered to Ginger. "We're actually at a football game. For the first time, I really feel like a genuine high school student full of that good old school spirit." I leaped up in my seat as the players collapsed in a heap on the field. "Yeah, Mesa. Go team. Do it again!" I yelled.

"Roni, they just sacked our quarterback," Ginger said.

"Oh. I knew that," I said, turning bright red. "I was just practicing my spirit."

"Well, don't fall off the bleachers while you're doing it," Ginger said, grabbing my jacket. "You've already demonstrated to Drew that you can be a klutz sometimes."

"You're right," I said, sitting down hurriedly. "Now

I want him to see me as gorgeous and spirited."

Ginger and Justine started giggling. Karen wasn't with us. She had a final rehearsal for tomorrow's recital. She had been so nervous at school all day that she'd hardly heard a word we said to her.

"Relax, Karen, you're going to do just fine," I'd told her, putting my arm around her shoulders. "We'll all be there."

"What if I screw up?"

"Nobody will notice except you. And if anyone says anything bad about you, I'll beat them up," I added, making a fist in her face until she finally smiled.

"Thanks, Roni," she said. "It means a lot to me, knowing that my friends support me."

"That's what friends are for, Karen," I said. "We helped Ginger get together with Ben. Ginger and Justine are coming to the football game with me tonight. Everything is going to turn out just great because we've got friend power going here!"

I slapped a high five with her.

"You're crazy," she'd said, but she'd laughed and the two frown lines had disappeared from her forehead.

Poor Karen, I thought now as I watched the football game. *It must be terrible to be so worried about failing and letting your parents down. I hope we can make things better for her.*

I stared at the figures on the field, trying to pick out Drew among the confusing mass of bodies. Then

131

I saw him, dancing his way through the defensive line before he was brought to the ground. "Doesn't Drew look great in his uniform?" I sighed.

"Ben looks good, too," Ginger said. "I hope he gets to play later in the varsity game. He says the coach has been treating him and Todd like rookies because they came from another school. They hardly got to play at all last week."

"At least that way they keep their uniforms clean," Justine commented. "I hate seeing messy uniforms."

Ginger looked across at me. "I don't think we have a real football fan here," she said.

"Remember they only had stuff like ballet and tennis at her old school," I said with a grin. "You don't get dirty doing those."

It wasn't a very exciting game, but it ended in a ten-seven victory for Alta Mesa. We were stiff and cold by the time we climbed down from the bleachers at the end.

"Do you realize we've got another whole game to watch after this?" Ginger moaned. "I don't know if I can sit for two more hours. Still, it will be worth suffering to ride home with Ben."

I didn't answer. I was trying to fight off the big disappointment that was growing in me. Drew was over with his team, surrounded by friends, unreachably far away. Any minute now he'd head for the locker room without even knowing I was here.

"Let's go get a hot chocolate, Roni," Ginger said.

I followed her like a zombie. I don't know what I'd expected to happen at the football game, but I'd been building it up in my mind as the most important night of my life. I'd told myself that this would be the night when Drew decided that I wasn't klutzy and weird, but sophisticated and spirited. Tonight, I'd thought, Roney with a *y* would take her rightful place as a fun, popular person. I'd even begun to believe in that stupid daydream where our eyes met across the end zone. Since I was sitting at midfield, this was hardly likely to happen, but I hadn't been able to shake off the feeling all evening that something miraculous was going to take place.

"I have to see Drew," I said suddenly. "That was the whole idea of coming tonight. I'll catch up with you guys down by the concession stand."

I sprinted after the disappearing team, determined to cut them off before they got to the locker room. Then I saw Drew. He was heading straight for me, in the middle of a big group as usual. But miraculously, Charlene wasn't with him.

This was my chance. It was now or never. But I couldn't think of anything to say! Drew was drawing near me. Soon he would pass by and be gone.

With a sudden flash of brilliance I remembered the Chinese jokes.

"Hey, Drew!" I yelled. "What do you call a Chinese fighter pilot?"

He looked across at me. I saw his eyes light up, and my heart jumped. "What?" he yelled back.

"One wing low!" I said.

"Good one." He laughed. "Where did you hear that?"

"I just made it up."

He nodded in approval.

Suddenly I realized I was standing in the middle of a group of laughing kids. I was the center of attention. I had made up that joke off the top of my head and it had been an instant success.

"All right, Roni," I heard someone say. "Got any more?"

"So you made it to the game," Drew said. He moved closer to me.

"Yeah. My friend's brother is giving us a ride home."

"Is he on the team?"

"Varsity. He's a junior. Todd Hartman."

"Oh, yeah? I've scrimmaged against him. He's new, isn't he?"

I nodded. "He just transferred here like we did when they changed the city boundary."

"That reminds me," Drew said. "I was out your way on Sunday, riding my friend's dirt bike. If I'd known your address, I'd have stopped by."

Suddenly I realized he was going to ask me for my address, right here, in front of everybody. Alarm bells started going off in my head. I didn't want this group of kids to know that I lived out on Old Adobe Road, in a Mexican neighborhood.

Miraculously, it was Charlene who saved me. Her high, clear voice cut through the crowd.

"Oh, there you are, Drew. I was waiting for you outside." Then she saw me. Instantly her flirtatious smile disappeared. "What happened this time?" she demanded. "Did she tackle you, or did she squirt the mustard from her hot dog all over you?"

"We were just talking, Charlene," Drew said.

She turned her freezing stare in my direction. "I don't think much of your taste, if this is who you choose to talk to these days. I know you're such a nice guy that you have to pay attention to all your many fans, but I'm kind of cold in this outfit. I want to go home."

"In a minute," Drew said.

"Now, Drew," Charlene said furiously.

"I said in a minute," Drew replied. "If you're cold, wait in the girls' locker room. I like hanging out with my friends after the game. It gives me a chance to wind down."

"Then I might just find somebody else to drive me home," Charlene said. "I'm sure there are many guys with nicer cars than yours just dying to give me a ride."

The tension in the air was so strong that I think I

stopped breathing. "Fine," Drew said at last. "If you want to go home with someone else, that's up to you."

"I will, then," Charlene snapped. She tossed back her bouncy blond curls and strode off in the direction of the parking lot.

"Now you've done it, Drew." One of the guys chuckled.

"Yeah, Drew, you're going to get it in the morning."

"She doesn't own me," Drew said angrily. "I don't always have to do what Charlene wants. She's getting to be a real pain."

I couldn't believe it. It looked like Drew and Charlene were actually breaking up before my eyes. My friends had thought I didn't have a chance with Drew because of Charlene, but she had just walked out on him. I was so astonished that it took a second for me to realize Drew was talking to me.

"Excuse me?" I said, reacting to his hand on my shoulder.

"I was thinking that we should do something this weekend," Drew said. "Do you want to come out for pizza tomorrow night with me and some of the guys?"

"Pizza with you?" I repeated. I couldn't believe my ears. This had to be a dream. It was too good to be real.

"Sure. Lombardi's, around seven? You want me to pick you up?"

"Uh . . . no. I might be in the city with my friends.

How about if I meet you there?"

"Okay. See you at seven, then. Bye, Roni."

"Bye, Drew."

I think I floated back to the concession stand.

"Did you talk to him?" Justine asked. "What did he say?"

"He asked me out tomorrow night."

"Yeah, right," Justine said, rolling her eyes at Ginger.

"No, I mean it," I said. "Drew invited me to go for pizza with him tomorrow night."

"You're kidding."

"I am dead serious."

"Wow, Roni. Drew really asked you on a date?" Justine said. "But what about Charlene?"

"You didn't see the little dramatic scene back there?" I asked. "She was mad because he was keeping her waiting, and he told her she didn't own him. Then she threw a fit and said she'd get someone else to drive her home."

"Roni, that's incredible!" Ginger yelled excitedly. "I can't believe it. You're actually going out with Drew Howard! Your magic really worked!"

We were all dancing around and hugging each other. When the varsity game started, I sat through the whole thing without even noticing the cold.

We were four happy people in the car on the ride home, too. Todd had gotten to play a lot, and the coach had said he'd done a good job. Coach had also told Ben that he'd try him as a wide receiver in practice, which made Ben happy. As I sat in the front seat beside Todd, wrapped in my own little cocoon of happiness, I kept glancing at Ginger and Ben. They sat together in the back seat, teasing each other and holding hands.

"Cut it out, you two," Todd called, glancing at them in the rearview mirror.

"Tell him to cut it out. He tickled me."

"Only because she took my glasses," Ben said.

"I didn't take your glasses. They're right here."

"Give them back, then. Ginger, stop it!"

There were more giggles. Todd looked across at me and sighed. "Do you think they've finally flipped?" he asked. "I mean, they were two fairly normal people until they got together. Now it's like being in kindergarten."

"Shut up, Todd. You're just jealous!" came Ginger's voice.

"Me? I wouldn't want to date Ben!"

I snuck a look at them, sitting close together and grinning happily. They seemed so right for each other. I kept thinking that tomorrow that would be Drew and me.

We were almost home when Ginger sat up straight in the back seat and said, "Roni. Tomorrow night is Karen's recital!"

"Oh, no! I was so excited, I forgot about it! Ginger, what am I going to do?"

"You'll have to tell Drew you can't go, I guess," Ginger said hesitantly.

"Tell Drew I can't go on a date with him? Are you totally out of your mind? Ginger, this is my dream come true."

"But Karen was counting on us all to be there, Roni," Ginger said.

"So, you and Justine are still going. She won't notice if one of us is missing."

"Yes, she will," Ginger said. "You promised her you'd go. She was especially counting on you. You know she feels close to you because you understand what she's going through."

I felt as if I were in a rapidly sinking elevator. "But Ginger, get real," I said. "Karen wouldn't expect me to give up a chance to go out with Drew. She'd understand how important this is to me."

"You have to do what you think is best," Ginger said quietly.

I wished she hadn't said that. I knew what I thought was best. I had given Karen a big speech about friends never letting each other down, and the best thing for me to do was go to the recital. But I also knew that there was no way I was going to turn down a chance to go out with Drew. *It's not as if I can really do anything for Karen,* I reasoned. I couldn't hold her bow or turn the pages of her music for her. I was just going to be a semi-visible blob in the audience. She probably wouldn't even be able to see me through the darkness. She might think I was there, even if I wasn't.

"Karen doesn't play till around nine," I said. "I could do both. Tell her I might be a little late."

"Okay," Ginger said. "I'll tell her."

I felt a distinct coldness as I got out of Todd's car at my door. But whether the coldness came from Ginger or from inside me, I couldn't tell.

12

To tell you the truth, I wasn't thinking much about Karen's recital as I got ready to meet Drew at Lombardi's Pizza. My brain was crammed with what I was going to say to him, how I was going to act, what it would be like if he kissed me. I had spent the entire afternoon trying on every outfit I owned. None of them seemed right for a night at Lombardi's with someone as cool as Drew Howard. I tried to think what Charlene would have worn, but then I decided that there was no way I could make myself into another Charlene. I wouldn't look right in cute little miniskirts and fluffy sweaters. I didn't own any, either.

In the end I decided on jeans and a plain white tank top. You can't go wrong with jeans, and this pair fit me really well. I decided I had better legs than

Charlene. Hers were kind of short and stumpy, I thought with satisfaction. Drew would notice that mine were much more attractive!

When I finally appeared in the living room, my whole family was there, watching TV and laughing loudly. I had told my parents that I was going out for pizza with a group of friends. I might have mentioned that there was a fantastic guy among them, but I had made the "group of friends" part very clear. I was sure they'd have a fit if they thought I was meeting a strange guy for a date.

"Is that what you're thinking of wearing out to a restaurant with a boy?" my mother demanded as soon as I entered the room.

I couldn't believe it—my mother knew exactly what was going on! It was amazing how she could see right through me. "Mama, it's a bunch of people going to a pizza place. You make it sound so fancy."

"It doesn't matter," she said. "Jeans are not for going out." Where had she been for the past twenty years?

"Mama, this is what everyone wears. I'll be fine."

"She's going out with a boy?" Abuela asked, sitting up in her chair to catch more of the conversation. She couldn't understand it all because my mother was speaking to me in Spanish, and I was answering her in English. We had been communicating like this for years and had gotten pretty good at it.

"With some friends, Abuela," I said.

"Male friends?"

"Of course."

"And who is to be the chaperon?"

"Oh, please, Abuela. This is America. You don't need a chaperon to eat pizza." I rolled my eyes to the ceiling. I was glad none of my friends was around to hear this.

"It's true, Mama," my father joined in. "The young people here have too much freedom, but that is the way things are. Roni's a good girl. I trust her."

I gave him a thankful smile. At least he was part of the twentieth century.

"And she's wearing trousers and an undershirt to go out in?" Abuela demanded. "Did you teach her that, Dolores?"

"No, Mama. But that's also the way things are in America."

"When I was young, we enjoyed dressing up in our best clothes," Abuela said. "Girls liked to look like girls in my day. We had clothes that we kept for special occasions—"

"That's right, Roni," my mother interrupted. "You have the perfect thing to wear tonight: the blouse Abuela brought for you."

"Excuse me?" I said.

"The pretty lace blouse. You look so nice in it. You said you were saving it for a special occasion. Go put it on," my mother said.

143

I could feel the color draining from my face. "Mama, there's no way I could wear a lacy Mexican blouse to a pizza parlor," I said. "Everyone would laugh at me."

"She doesn't like the blouse I brought for her?" Abuela asked.

"Of course she likes it. She's saving it for a special occasion. Go put it on, Roni."

I could just imagine Drew's face when he saw me in that blouse. He'd go running back to Charlene in a second. This was the time to put my foot down. "I'm sorry, Mama," I said, "but I'm not wearing the blouse tonight. I like what I'm wearing."

"But Roni—"

"Mom, you want me to fit in, don't you? Then don't make me look like a freak!" I snapped.

"Roni, what a terrible thing to say," Mama gasped.

My father held up his hand. "The girl is right, Dolores. She lives in America. She can't always look like an outsider."

"But I want her to be proud of her heritage, José," my mother said.

"Of course she's proud. She's also realistic enough to know that she has to blend in. Now go and have a good time, daughter."

I went over and kissed his forehead. "Thank you, Papa," I said.

❀   ❀   ❀

I remembered Karen's recital as I rode into the city on the bus. A jolt of guilt shot through my body. What if she messed up because I wasn't there? What if she hated me forever because of this and the others hated me, too? What if they all felt I'd let them down? Both Ginger and Justine had called me earlier in the day, and they both said that they understood I wanted to be with Drew. But I could sense a coldness in their voices, as if they didn't really understand at all. I felt as if both of them would have made a different choice in my situation. When I said that I'd try to get there before Karen played, they both said, "Uh-huh," as if they didn't believe that I'd try at all.

I began to feel really bad about letting Karen down. Then I came up with a great idea. Maybe Drew and I could leave the pizza parlor and stop by to see the end of the recital before we went somewhere fun. That way Karen would know I hadn't forgotten about her, and I'd be able to stomp out all those guilty thoughts that were still whispering at the back of my mind.

Lombardi's Pizza was bright and noisy. I'd seen it before, but I'd never been inside. Lots of kids from school hung out there. Tonight it was full—eight of us had to cram into a booth meant for six. Besides Drew and me there were two girls and four guys. The other girls looked at me oddly, as if I were a Martian who had dropped into their midst. They were both cheerleaders, probably Charlene's friends. Obviously they couldn't understand what I was doing with Drew.

I was scrunched in between Drew and a guy named Brett. I could feel Drew's leg touching mine, and it sent shivers all over me. I wondered if it made him feel the same way. He was obviously having a good time, being as loud and funny as ever and making us all laugh with his stories. As he leaned forward to say something to the kids across the table, he actually slipped his arm around my shoulders.

I felt like I was in heaven. I was in the middle of the most popular group in the school, and I was sitting with Drew's arm around my shoulders. At this moment, all the horrible things that had happened since I conjured up Drew were worth it. I'd willingly have put up with any number of embarrassing incidents just to be here, carefree and laughing with Drew beside me, while all the other girls in the place looked at us enviously.

After we'd been there about an hour, a group of kids took over the booth next to ours. They were clearly Latinas, speaking Spanish and dressed in the sort of clothes my mother always wanted me to wear. One of the girls was even wearing a frilly Mexican blouse like the one Abuela gave me. I shuddered and picked up my slice of pizza.

But it seemed I wasn't the only one who had noticed them. Brett leaned across me. "Hey, Drew, look who just came in," he said with a big grin on his face. "It's Chiquita Banana!"

"*Ay, caramba,*" said the guy sitting across from me.

One of the other guys made a high-pitched trilling noise to get the girls' attention.

"Sorry, but they don't serve bean pizzas here," Brett called.

I saw one of the girls in the next booth flush and look down.

"Hey, Drew, what's a Mexican's idea of a picnic?" one of the guys across the table yelled. Before Drew could answer, the guy finished, "Beans and rice at the border."

The kids at the next table could hear everything the boys were saying, but they were pretending that they couldn't. They were trying to carry on a normal conversation, but the strained smiles on their faces showed me how upset they really were. I heard one of the girls say in Spanish, "Just ignore them."

Everyone at my table was laughing and making jokes about wetbacks and coyotes and beaners. A red haze of anger was growing in my head. I understood now how Karen had felt about the Chinese jokes at school. I couldn't believe I had ever thought it was okay to make fun of any ethnic group. It was mean and small and wrong.

Suddenly I realized something else. I might want to act just like all the other kids. I might wish I was

147

blond and popular like Charlene. But I was stuck with my ancestry, and I was proud of who I was. I was proud of my family's heritage, and furious that anyone would make fun of it. It could have been me or my parents or one of my little sisters sitting at that next booth.

I glanced at Drew. He hadn't said anything, but he was smiling. And he wasn't stopping his friends from telling the jokes. I got to my feet.

"Let me out of here, please," I said to Drew.

His smile disappeared as soon as he saw my face. "Roni, what's wrong?" he asked.

"You are, that's what," I said. "All of you are very wrong. You think it's funny to run down everyone else's culture, don't you? You think you're so superior."

"What are you talking about? They're just harmless jokes."

"Not if you're on the receiving end of them."

"They're Mexicans," Brett said. "They can't even understand us."

"They understand perfectly," I said.

"How do you know?"

"Because I'm Mexican, too. I can understand what they've been saying. And what they've been saying is to ignore you because you are ignorant and don't know any better," I said. "Now let me out of here, please. I don't want to be around people who get their fun from putting down anyone who is different from them."

As I pushed past Drew I heard one of the guys saying, "He sure picked the wrong girl to make Charlene mad. She's more trouble than Charlene was."

Then it dawned on me what a fool I had been. Drew hadn't invited me out because he wanted to get to know me better. He had done it because he knew it would make Charlene jealous and he wanted to pay her back for the fight they'd had. Tears of anger and embarrassment stung my eyes as I headed for the door.

Drew came after me and grabbed my arm. "Roni, wait," he said. "Look, I'm sorry. I didn't realize you were Mexican."

"That's because I tried to keep it from you," I said. "I wanted to feel like I belonged in your crowd, and I wanted you to like me. But now I realize that it's more important to like myself. It shouldn't matter to you whether or not I'm Mexican—you shouldn't make fun of anyone's culture, ever, no matter who you're with. I can't go along with what you've been doing."

"I understand," he said. "My friends don't mean any harm."

"They cause harm whether they mean it or not. And you were smiling, too," I said. "You didn't stop them. Besides, I'm not a rubber ball. You can't keep

149

using me for whatever you want and expect me to come bouncing back."

"What are you talking about?"

"I'm not totally stupid," I said. Tears were running down my cheeks now. "You only asked me here to get back at Charlene, didn't you? Well, thanks for the pizza, but I've got to go. There's a violin recital that I'm already late for."

I shook my arm loose from his grip and ran out of Lombardi's into the night.

I really didn't know where I was going. I just kept walking and walking, staring straight ahead of me. I had to get to Karen's recital before it was too late, but I wasn't sure if the buses were still running. I didn't even know exactly how to get there. It hurt too much to think anyway, so I just kept walking. The sound of my feet slapping against the sidewalk and the cold wind on my face were all I could handle right now.

Cars sped past. One of them honked at me. Slowly I realized that I was alone in a big city and that it was dark. *Not too smart, Roni,* I thought. In fact, I was asking for trouble. I wondered if I had enough on me for a taxi, but I was scared to stop in the middle of a dark street and count my money. Maybe I could promise to pay the driver when I got to the recital. Justine always had loads of money on her.

A car slowed down behind me, its headlights throwing my shadow against the brick wall of the

150

building next to me. *Keep walking, Roni,* I told my-self. The whole street was deserted, but the bright lights of a populated street were straight ahead. If I could just get there, I'd be fine.

I resisted the temptation to run. Determined to show the driver I wasn't scared of him, I held my head high and kept on walking. The headlights inched closer. The car was even with me now. I could hear its engine rumbling. A door opened.

"Get in, Roni," Drew's voice said.

I thought I would faint with relief. "It's okay. I'm going to my friend's music recital," I told Drew. "I should have been there all along, but I let her down just for the chance to be with you. Shows how dumb I am, right?"

"Roni, please get in. I'm holding up traffic," Drew said.

"I said I'm okay. Go back to your friends. I don't belong with you."

"Will you get in or am I going to have to drag you inside?" he yelled.

I got in.

"Boy, you are the toughest person in the world to apologize to," Drew said.

"You don't have to apologize," I said.

"I want to apologize, you dummy," Drew said. "I feel really bad about what happened. The more I think about it, the more I realize you were right. It's

151

too easy to go along with things that make you feel uncomfortable. I'd never put myself on the other end before, but you're right, those jokes weren't funny at all. Will you forgive me?"

I nodded. "I forgive you," I said. "But I'm not going back there. If you'll drop me at a bus stop, I'll head over to my friend's recital. I might just make it in time."

"Where is it?"

"Over in Tempe."

"There won't be a bus at this time of night," he said. "I'll drive you."

"You don't have to. Your friends are all back at the pizza parlor."

He gave me an exasperated look. "I want to, Roni. Understand? Where is it?"

I told him the address, and we sped through the night in silence. The wind was cold on my face. I was finally riding beside Drew—on a real date, just like in my fantasy. But it didn't feel like a fantasy anymore. I couldn't forget that he had used me, and it hurt.

"What kind of music is the recital for?" he asked after a long silence.

"Violin."

"Oh, great, my favorite," he said in a bright voice that was intended to make me smile. "Come on, cheer up," he said. "Everything's going to be okay."

When I didn't answer, he added, "I said I was sorry. You're not still mad at me, are you?"

"I guess I'm mainly mad at myself," I said slowly. "I let myself believe things that just weren't possible."

"Like what?"

"That you were asking me out because you liked me, not because you wanted to get back at Charlene."

"I must admit that annoying Charlene was my first reason," Drew said with a smile. "I knew she'd be furious if she found out, and I wanted to teach her a lesson. We've been going out so long, she's started to act like I belong to her."

I nodded.

"I'm my own person," Drew said. "I don't want to come running because some girl snaps her fingers."

"Of course not."

"You wouldn't be like that, would you?" he asked. "I mean, you might hit me with a book, or shoot ketchup at me, but you'd never snap your fingers."

I laughed.

"You're not like any girl I've met before, Roni," he said.

"I know I'm weird. You don't have to say it," I said.

"You're weird in a nice way. You're your own person. You're not trying to be just like everyone else. I like that," he said. "I guess that's why I've been thinking about you so much. I'm the kind of person who gets bored easily, but I don't think I'd ever be bored around you. I never know what you're going to do next."

"You've been thinking about me?" I asked in astonishment.

"I sure have, ever since you commandeered my car to chase a Volvo. You made me laugh. You made me think, I bet that girl would be fun to be with. Dangerous, but fun."

"I'm not usually dangerous," I said. "It just seems to happen when you're around."

"Maybe it's not so bad. You certainly got my attention," he said. "And you've made me think that maybe I've been going with Charlene too long."

"Really?"

Drew turned into the tree-lined streets of Tempe. "I mean, do you know what Charlene would have done if I'd gotten ice cream all over her? She'd have called me every name under the sun." He pulled the car to a halt under a tree. "You're some girl, Roni. I really like you."

Then he took my chin in his fingers and pulled my face gently toward his. His lips met mine in a warm, tender kiss.

I had pictured this moment a zillion times in my life, but the reality was way more perfect than the dream had been. The thought shot through my head: *I'm kissing Drew Howard in a red convertible!* But then I closed my eyes and I didn't think anymore. My whole body was tingling and I felt like I was floating in a perfect, crystal bubble—just Drew and me in our own little world.

Chapter

13

I wanted the kiss to go on forever, but suddenly I remembered Karen's recital. I jumped away from Drew.

"Drew, we have to get going or my friend will already have played," I said.

"Oh, yeah, I almost forgot," he said with a grin. "Something distracted me. Okay, I'll step on the gas."

The red car shot away through the dark, leafy streets. I was sitting close to Drew now, so close that my shoulder was touching his. He put his arm around me.

"Uh, don't you think you need two hands to drive?" I asked.

He shook his head. "So tell me, Roni, was that your first kiss?" he asked.

"The first one that counted. Did I do okay?"

"Pretty good, for a beginner. But are you telling me that you've been with other guys before?" He pretended to be shocked.

"If you count some dweeb at the seventh-grade dance. He only came up to my shoulder and he was wearing braces. It was not a memorable experience."

Drew laughed. "So I'm definitely an improvement?"

"Are you kidding? That was the most perfect thing that ever happened to me."

He looked pleased as he stopped the car at the music conservatory. "Maybe we can go for a soda or something after the recital. Is it going to go on long?"

"Oh, I think Karen is scheduled to play all twenty-nine movements of Beethoven's last symphony," I said, trying to keep a straight face.

"All twenty-nine?" Drew cried, horrified. "Are there really twenty-nine movements in a symphony?"

I burst out laughing, and Drew grabbed my shoulders. "I'll get you for that!" he said, his eyes twinkling.

This was what I had always dreamed about—this easy togetherness with a boy. I didn't know what to expect on Monday morning, when I had to face Charlene at school. I didn't even know if Drew would go back to her in the end, but tonight I didn't care. Tonight he was with me, and that was all that mattered.

Three little kids were playing a violin trio as we went in. The sounds they made were only slightly more pleasant than those of a cat having its tail

157

twisted, but they were giving it their all, moving their bows up and down with serious little faces. They finished to loud applause. Drew and I slipped into the back row as the music teacher came onstage.

"And now it gives me great pleasure to present Miss Karen Nguyen, who will play one of Bach's Brandenburg Concertos," she said.

Karen stood and made her way to the stage. She was dressed in a black skirt and a white blouse, and her face was deathly pale. She almost stumbled as she came onstage to polite applause.

I couldn't stand it any longer. I jumped up in my seat. "All right, Karen, you can do it! Yeah!" I yelled. Disapproving faces turned to stare at me, but I didn't care. I watched a grin spread across Karen's face as she picked up her violin and set it under her chin.

The moment she started playing, I knew we didn't have to worry about her. Pure, sweet music flowed out of her violin. Her bow flew over the strings, and her fingers danced like butterflies.

"Hey, she's pretty good," Drew whispered in my ear.

Good wasn't the word for it. She was brilliant. Everyone in the room sat entirely still while she played. When she finished, there was a burst of enthusiastic applause. People got to their feet. I felt a lump in my throat, almost as if this had been my great moment, not hers. Karen looked embarrassed but pleased as she took her bow.

The music teacher said some closing words, and then the audience began to file out of the concert hall. I stood in the back, watching people surround Karen to congratulate her. She talked to them all with a polite smile on her face, but as soon as she could she pushed through the crowd and came running back to me.

"Roni, you came after all!" she cried, flinging her arms around me. "Ginger and Justine were sure you wouldn't make it, but I knew you'd come. I'm so happy. I couldn't have done it without you!"

"Sure you could. You were fantastic, Karen. You're just like a professional."

"I'm not that good yet," she said. "I made some mistakes—"

"Oh, yeah, tons of mistakes that we all noticed," I teased her. "You sounded incredible to me. I'm so proud to be your friend. Can I have your autograph before you become too famous to give it to me?"

She laughed and gave me a friendly shove. "Get out of here," she said.

Ginger and Justine appeared behind her. "You were so good!" Justine yelled as Ginger hugged Karen. Then they both turned to me.

"So you came after all, Roni," Ginger said. "I

didn't think you would. I couldn't believe it when I heard your voice back there."

"That was nice of you, Roni," Justine added. "I know how much it must have meant to you to leave Drew."

"Who said anything about leaving Drew?" I said. "He came with me."

Three pairs of eyes turned to see Drew standing over by the wall, waiting for me. He grinned that wonderful, confident, wicked smile of his.

"I'm tough. I knew I could suffer through it if she could," he said. "Those little kids, I mean," he added hastily, glancing at Karen. "I don't know anything about Bach, but you sounded pretty good to me. Now, if you could only learn to play some cool stuff. Do you know any Pearl Jam?"

"Drew, shut up," I said, slapping his arm.

The others looked at me with interest. I could tell they were dying to ask questions, but I wasn't about to say anything now.

"My parents are taking us out for ice cream, if you'd like to come," Karen said.

I looked up at Drew.

"Thanks, but Roni and I have other plans," he said. "Ready to split, Roni? We'll see you guys later."

He took my hand—in front of all those people, in front of my three best friends, he actually took my hand. I could feel the warmth going all the way up my arm. I thought I might actually die of happiness! I gave my friends one last, blissful smile as we went out into the night.

It was one very happy person who finally came home at ten-thirty. Drew and I had stopped off at Cactus Lanes and bowled for an hour, and I beat him once. Then he drove me home—all the way home, right up to my front gate. "Hey, you don't live far from me at all," he said. "That's great."

"Someday you'll have to meet my parents," I said. But not now. I wasn't ready for that yet. Abuela would probably ask him what his prospects were and how many children he wanted!

"Yeah, some other time," he said, grinning. In the darkness outside my house he kissed me again, and it was as sweet and wonderful as the first time.

I knew my friends would be on the phone early the next morning wanting to know all the details. Although I didn't mind talking about Drew one bit, I didn't want to go through the same story three times. Then it occurred to me that I could just ask them all over for dinner. My mother had been telling me to invite my friends home ever since school started. I finally felt like doing it.

As soon as I woke up on Sunday, I went into the kitchen and asked Mama if the girls could come over that night. She looked really pleased. "How nice,

Roni," she said. "We've been looking forward to entertaining your friends."

I ran to the phone and called Ginger, Karen, and Justine. They were all really excited. "I love Mexican food," Justine said. "And I can't wait to play with your little brother again."

Karen sounded a little hesitant. "Are you sure, Roni?" she asked. "I mean, your grandmother is visiting right now, which must be extra work for your mother . . . and I got the feeling when we were at your house last week that you didn't really want us there."

"Of course I want you," I said, blushing now at my own stupidity. How could I be dumb enough to think my friends wouldn't like me anymore if they saw my house?

"I'll come over and help get things ready if you want," Ginger said. "That way I can get the scoop on you and Drew before anyone else. Just think of it, Roni. You and Drew Howard. Did you ever, in your wildest dreams, imagine it would happen?"

"Of course," I said, grinning to myself. "I invented him, remember? He was the perfect boy I had my spirits conjure up."

Ginger laughed. "You and your spirits," she said. "Just don't levitate the tablecloth tonight."

"You just be careful that you don't bug me," I said. "Who knows what I might get my spirits to do to you?"

I hung up the phone and turned to see my mother hovering nervously behind me. "Do you think we should play it safe and just barbecue hamburgers for them in case they don't like Mexican food?" she asked.

"Of course not," I said. "It's the Mexican food they're coming for. I want them to see what real Mexican food tastes like—not that wishy-washy stuff you get in fast-food places."

Mama's face lit up. "We'll ask Abuela to make her special enchiladas," she said. "And I could do chicken with mole. I bet they've never tried that before."

"I'm not sure if they'll like that," I said cautiously. Mole is made with dark chocolate and it tastes kind of unusual.

"It doesn't matter. It will be a new experience for them," Mama said. "It's always good to try new things. If they don't like the mole, we know they'll love Abuela's enchiladas."

"You'd better ask her right now if she'll make them," I said. "You know how long it takes to prepare everything from scratch. She'll probably want us to milk a cow to make the cheese!"

Mama laughed and said I was a terrible child, but she did go to ask Abuela. I followed her to the back patio, where Abuela was sitting in the rocking chair.

"Mama, we have a favor to ask," my mother said, bending over Abuela. "Roni has some friends coming to dinner for a real Mexican meal. We hoped you'd make those special enchiladas for them."

"Which ones?" Abuela asked.

"You know, with the green chilies and lots of cheese, Abuela," I said. "They're really good."

"Oh, yes," she said. "I haven't made them for so long, I might have forgotten the recipe."

"You don't make them anymore?" Mama asked.

"I haven't made them in years. Not since they started making such good frozen ones. You can buy all sorts of stuff frozen now, you know." She wagged a finger at my mother. "You should look into them, Dolores. It would save you all that time you spend slaving in the kitchen right now. You're working your-self to death, cooking everything from scratch. Nobody does that anymore."

I started giggling helplessly.

"What's wrong with the child?" Abuela asked.

I saw my mother fighting to keep a straight face.

"Nothing, Abuela," I said. "Nothing at all."

Then I had a great thought. "If it's supposed to be a Mexican meal, Abuela, I can wear your blouse." My friends would understand that I was looking weird to make my grandmother happy. And Abuela did look delighted at my suggestion.

I went into my room and put on the blouse. Then I glanced at myself in the mirror and did a double take. A new, different person was looking back at me—not

Roni Ruiz, confident American teenager, but Veronica Consuela, who might have worn a lace mantilla and danced to guitars and gone to bullfights. It was a part of myself I had never paid much attention to before. I knew from now on I'd be a lot more interested in hearing what my parents had to say about the old country. After all, it was my heritage, too!

I came out of my room just as Ginger was coming in the back door.

"Here I am, all ready to help," she called. "I've got my sunglasses in case I have to cut up a million onions and chili peppers and I've—" She stopped, her mouth open. "Wow, Roni. Is that the blouse you were talking about?"

"I don't own two blouses like this," I said, grinning sheepishly.

"It looks great on you," Ginger said. "It makes you look so grown up and . . . sexy."

"Sexy?"

"Yeah," she said. "You better be careful if you wear it around Drew!"

Karen and Justine also thought the blouse looked good on me, although Justine said it was a shame I didn't have it last year, when the Southwest look was really in.

My mother had put the big trestle table out on the patio, under the grapevine. It was cool out, and the air smelled sweet as we sat down to dinner. Even

Paco behaved perfectly, politely talking to my friends in English.

In the middle of the meal Abuela touched my arm. "Roni," she whispered, "I've just noticed something."

"Yes, Abuela?"

"Your friends. They're not Mexican, are they?"

I remembered that she had been asleep the last time they were over. I looked from Ginger's freckles to Justine's blond ponytail to Karen's almond-shaped eyes, and I started to laugh. "No, Abuela, they're not Mexican," I said.

"Good," she said, nodding. "You judge people by their personalities, not their cultures. That's how it should be."

"You're right, Abuela," I said. "Lately I've decided that friendship is more than skin deep."

About the Author

Janet Quin-Harkin has written over fifty books for teenagers, including the bestseller *Ten-Boy Summer*. She is the author of the *Friends* series, the *Heartbreak Cafe* series, and the *Senior Year* series. She has also written several romances.

Ms. Quin-Harkin lives with her husband in San Rafael, California. She has four children. In addition to writing books, she teaches creative writing at a nearby college.

Here's a sneak preview of The Boyfriend Club™ #3:

Karen's Perfect Match

"Please come to the computer lab with us," Walter said. "I've created a new program—"

"Which should be of special interest to you girls," Ronald interrupted, "seeing that you have your Boyfriend Club."

Roni, Ginger, Justine, and I were speechless with horror. We had thought that the Boyfriend Club was our own little secret. Now we were surrounded by Nerds who knew all about it. "What are you talking about?" I asked.

"It is our understanding that you are all members of a Boyfriend Club," Walter said seriously, "the object of which is to help each other get dates."

"Who told you that?" Ginger demanded.

"We . . . sort of . . . overheard," Ronald confessed.

"You spied on us?" Justine gasped.

168

"I wouldn't put it that way," Ronald said. "We just happened to be following you girls and overheard you talking about your club. But please don't worry. Your secret will be safe with us."

"In fact," Walter said, "we've been working very hard on your behalf. We actually devoted the last meeting of the Computer Club to making life easier for you."

"Walter, what are you talking about?" Roni demanded.

Walter blushed. "We've created a program for you," he said.

"What kind of program?" Justine asked.

"To come up with a perfect match," Walter said proudly. "We've entered the information on hundreds of guys into our database, including whether they're available or not. Now all we have to do is feed in *your* information and bingo! We fix you up with the perfect guy."

We weren't giggling anymore.

"Are you serious?" Justine asked.

"Come to the lab," Ronald said. "I think you'll be impressed. Walter is really hot stuff with databases."

"Are you sure this thing isn't rigged so that it fixes us up with you guys?" Justine asked suspiciously.

"Certainly not," Walter said. "We're serious scientists. We don't rig our experiments."

We looked at each other. Finally Justine grabbed my arm. "Come on, Karen," she said. "Roni and Ginger have boyfriends, but if you and I don't meet some new boys, we'll be going to the Homecoming Dance with each other!"

"Are you crazy?" Ginger demanded.

"I know it's a scary thought," Justine said, "but maybe it's worth the risk. The Nerds could really fix us up with the dates of our dreams."

"Date of your nightmares, if I know the Nerds," Roni said.

"Well, I think it's worth a try. Don't you, Karen?" Justine asked.

I nodded. "It's *definitely* worth a try," I said, following Walter toward the computer lab.

When we got there, Walter sat down at the computer. "Who wants to be first?" he asked.

Justine looked at me. "Karen does," she said, pushing me forward.

"Okay, Karen, tell me about yourself."

"I'm not sure what I'm like. Just ordinary," I said. "Quiet, sort of shy around strangers . . ."

"Fun when you get to know her," Roni added. "Great sense of humor. Fantastic violin player."

"What are you, her PR person?" Justine demanded.

"She's too modest to say good things about herself," Roni said. "I know Karen."

"So I'll put music as a primary interest. Right, Karen?" Walter asked.

"I guess," I said. "Put down all kinds of music. I don't like only classical, you know. I like rock as much as anyone else does."

"What other interests?"

170

"Reading," I said. "Movies . . . I don't know what else. I don't do much. I must be a boring person."

"No, you're not," Roni said fiercely. "You haven't been allowed to do many things yet because of your music. But you are definitely not boring, Karen."

"What characteristics are you looking for in a guy?" Walter asked.

"Tall, dark, and handsome. What else is there?" Justine cracked.

I smiled. "Sounds good to me," I said. "Nice personality. Easy to talk to. That's all I really want. After all, this will be a first dating opportunity for me. I'm kind of shy around boys."

"But that doesn't mean she wants a real wimpy dork," Roni interrupted. I was glad she'd said that. I would've said it myself, but I thought the Nerds might take it personally.

"All right," Walter said. "Let's run it."

The screen went blank. Then a name appeared. SEAN BAXTER.

"Sean Baxter!" I exclaimed.

"Sean Baxter?" Roni repeated. "Do you know him?"

"Not to talk to," I said. "I know who he is, though. He plays oboe in the orchestra."

"Is he cute?" Justine asked.

"Yeah. I guess he is kind of cute," I said. "Dark-haired. Serious looking. Wears glasses. Quiet."

"Sounds just right for you, Karen," Ginger said.

171

"Let me check the compatibility factor," Walter said, tapping in some more commands.

The words appeared on the screen: COMPATIBILITY FACTOR: 9.

"That's incredible," Owen said excitedly.

"What does it mean?" I asked.

"It means that on a scale of one to ten, you and Sean Baxter are ninety percent compatible. An almost perfect match!"

"Wow!" I said. I was trying to picture Sean's face, trying to imagine him as somebody just right for me.

"So what does Karen do now?" Justine asked impatiently.

"That's up to her," Walter said. "I just match you up with guys. I don't set up the dates."

"That's a lot of help," Justine snapped. "How are we supposed to get her together with Sean? She can't just walk across the orchestra room and say, 'Hi, the computer says we're ninety percent compatible, so how about a date?'"

I laughed nervously. "I can't see myself doing that," I said. "I'd never have the nerve to go up and speak to him out of the blue."

"Of course not," Roni said. "If he's compatible with you, he's probably a little shy, too—he'd be very embarrassed. This is a job for the Boyfriend Club!"

You don't need
—— a boyfriend to join! ——

Now you and your friends can join the real Boyfriend Club and receive a special Boyfriend Club kit filled with lots of great stuff only available to Boyfriend Club members.

- **A mini phone book for your special friends' phone numbers**
- **A cool Boyfriend Club pen**
- **A really neat pocket-sized mirror and carrying case**
- **A terrific change purse/keychain**
- **A super doorknob hanger for your bedroom door**
- **The exclusive Boyfriend Club Newsletter**
- **A special Boyfriend Club ID card**

All this for just $3.50!

If you join today, you'll receive your special package and be an official member in 4-6 weeks. Just fill in the coupon below and mail to: The Boyfriend Club, Dept. B, Troll Associates, 100 Corporate Drive, Mahwah, NJ 07430

- -

☐ **Yes,** I want to be a member of the real Boyfriend Club. I have enclosed a check or money order for $3.50 payable to The Boyfriend Club.

Name_____

Address_____

City_____State_____Zip_____

Age_____Where did you buy this book?_____

Sorry, this offer is only available in the U.S.

The Boyfriend Club™

ADVICE EXCHANGE

Boyfriend Club Central asked:

What should you do when you don't like your best friend's new friend?

And you said:

Don't hang out with your best friend when she's with her new friend.

— Amy L., Baltimore, MD

Call her on the phone and try to get to know her better.

— Jamie V., Paramus, NJ

Invite the new friend to spend time with both of you. Maybe you'll get to like her in time.

— Fran S., Long Island, NY

Try to figure out what you really don't like about her. You might just be jealous.

- Caroline P., Nyack, NY

Tell your best friend how you feel.

- Dottie D., San Diego, CA

Make sure you have other friends—don't spend all your free time with just your best friend. - Julie K., Canton, OH

If you're nice to her, she'll be nice to you. Then you can all be friends.

- Vicky A., Reno, NV

Now we want to know:
What should you do when you want to date but your parents say you're not old enough?

Write and tell us what you think, and you may see your advice in the next ADVICE EXCHANGE:

Boyfriend Club Central
Dept. B
Troll Associates
100 Corporate Drive
Mahwah, NJ 07430